11/19

"There's a saying in county Kerry."

Caitlin slanted an amused glance at Jake as she went on. "That no one has ever had a victory over the Irish people. All would-be victors find themselves gloriously lost in the arms of our women."

"Very subtle. Such a saving on blood. So," Jake asked, "my ancestor lived happily ever after in the arms of an Irish colleen?"

She sighed. "No. He was hanged in Killarney by the Cromwellians."

"It sounds as if he'd have been wiser to spurn the seductive women and keep his life and self-respect by sticking to his original job."

"That's very unromantic of you!" she declared.

"But wise," he said sardonically. "It's a lesson to be remembered I think, if you're anything like the women around here."

D0057302

Sara Wood lives in a rambling sixteenth-century home in the medieval town of Lewes amid the Sussex hills. Her sons have claimed the cellar for bikes, making ferret cages, taxidermy and winemaking, while Sara has virtually taken over the study with her reference books, word processor and what have you. Her amiable, tolerant husband, she says, squeezes in wherever he finds room. After having tried many careers—secretary, guest house proprietor, play-group owner and primary teacher—she now finds writing romance novels gives her enormous pleasure.

Books by Sara Wood

Don't miss any of our special offers. Write to us at the following address for information on our newest releases.

Harlequin Reader Service
901 Fuhrmann Blvd., P.O. Box 1397, Buffalo, NY 14240
Canadian address: P.O. Box 603,
Fort Erie, Ont. L2A 5X3

MASTER OF CASHEL

Sara Wood

Harlequin Books

TORONTO • NEW YORK • LONDON
AMSTERDAM • PARIS • SYDNEY • HAMBURG
STOCKHOLM • ATHENS • TOKYO • MILAN

Original hardcover edition published in 1989
by Mills & Boon Limited

ISBN 0-373-03066-5

Harlequin Romance first edition July 1990

Copyright © 1989 by Sara Wood.
All rights reserved. Except for use in any review, the reproduction or utilization
of this work in whole or in part in any form by any electronic, mechanical or
other means, now known or hereafter invented, including xerography,
photocopying and recording, or in any information storage or retrieval system,
is forbidden without the permission of the publisher, Harlequin Enterprises
Limited, 225 Duncan Mill Road, Don Mills, Ontario, Canada M3B 3K9.

All the characters in this book have no existence outside the imagination of
the author and have no relation whatsoever to anyone bearing the same name
or names. They are not even distantly inspired by any individual known or
unknown to the author, and all incidents are pure invention.

® are Trademarks registered in the United States Patent and Trademark Office
and in other countries.

Printed in U.S.A.

CHAPTER ONE

JAKE FERRITER was coming home. Not to his birth-place—that was Florida—and not to Switzerland, where he'd been educated in a series of international schools. Even his working life had failed to give him a sense of belonging somewhere, since his job meant a nomadic existence. Home, to him, was a place he'd never even visited, never even heard of until two years ago. Home was Cashelkerry.

No Ferriter had set foot on Cashel land since his great-grandfather's time. Yet it belonged to him and he felt that with a passion that surprised him. It was his ancestral home, and a force more powerful than mere pride or a sense of ownership held him in its grip, making him—a tough, hardened and cynical man of the world—fall into reverie as he imagined past and future generations of the Ferriter family striding the land.

But every paradise and every dream has a flaw. The snag with Cashel was that someone was already living there. Before he could take possession, he had to carry out an eviction.

Relishing the prospect of reclaiming his rights from the intruder, Jake's jaw jutted forwards and his foot pressed firmly on the accelerator, thrusting the open-top car effortlessly past a cruising Mercedes. The road stretched wide and empty ahead. In sheer exhilaration at being free from all responsibilities—however temporarily—he continued to accelerate in the Maserati until the wind was tearing at his neat black hair and his face tingled, the smooth skin more used to a tropical sun than the fresh clean bite of Southern Ireland's air. When he finally slowed, he found that he'd been grinning, something he hadn't done much of lately. In fact, he couldn't remember how long it had been since he felt so intoxicated with life.

A flicked glance in the driving mirror told him something else; his once dead eyes now glinted with their old dark, wicked green light. Women had weakened in the blaze of his predatory hunger; business competitors flinched from the fierce intensity of his unwavering laser-like stare.

'Jake Ferriter,' he murmured into the wind, 'life begins again with a vengeance!'

First would come a highly satisfying battle with the O'Connell girl, followed by an equally pleasurable victory, and then, at last, the opportunity to realise his dreams. Jake laughed aloud in delight, unable to restrain his exuberance.

He drove slowly through Killarney, stopping only to pick up a newspaper and smiling inwardly at the stares he attracted. There weren't many men striding purposefully through Killarney in dark, French-cut business suits, and certainly none who were tall and strikingly attractive, exuding the urgent drive of a man with a mission and the sure knowledge of its success.

After a while he became irritated by his slightly uneven pace. Few onlookers, however, even noticed that he had an imperceptible limp. Jake did his utmost to force a balanced, fast stride. Already there had been a marked improvement. Soon there would be no visible memory left. His face darkened and then his jaw thrust out again in a characteristic determination. He'd eliminate with typical ruthlessness that small, infuriatingly persistent reminder of the last year, by persevering in the punishing physical programme he had devised for himself.

A devilish smile played about his lips as he slid his lithe body into the dusty red car. It was his favourite colour, the colour of action and assertiveness. He'd driven over three hundred miles since dawn, and the Maserati looked in worse shape than he did! Oh, he was in fine form at last. The pleasure of being fit again, and close to his destination—plus the prospect of a fight— made his adrenalin surge.

Jake's smile broadened and his perfect teeth flashed in a piratical grin at the thought of his intentions. He almost felt sorry for Caitlin O'Connell! Poor unsuspecting girl. She wouldn't know what had hit her!

'I'm just going down to the long-house.'

Caitlin spoke to the hefty red-headed man sitting at her father's desk. She'd popped her head around the study door and it had given her a jolt to see someone different in the big leather chair. Her face smoothed into a blank mask. It was no use letting her emotions take over; there was too much to do.

'We'll work through the household accounts when I get back,' she said firmly.

Cormac Kelly nodded, his strong face troubled. Caitlin hoped he wouldn't make assumptions about the way she was relying on him at the moment. As her father's estate manager, he had once proposed marriage. She made her eyes remote. Just because she was alone now, and in financial difficulties, he needn't think she wanted to be dependent on a man. She wasn't a fluttery kind of woman. Besides, every bit of her energy needed to be concentrated on Cashel. Marriage and men could wait; she was still only twenty-two.

'I'll have everything ready,' he said gently. 'Are you sure you don't want me to work things out for you? There's no need for you to worry yourself with details. I'm willing to handle everything.'

'I know,' she said gratefully, softening slightly. Cormac was a good man, steady and reliable. 'But I want to know exactly where I stand. I want to get rid of my image as a jet setter with a silver spoon in my mouth. That hurt, Cormac. And the worst thing is that it's partially true.'

He frowned and glanced at the *Kerry Times*, with its scurrilous article about the debts of Seamus O'Connell and the imaginative report on his bereaved daughter.

'You're nothing like the way the papers portrayed you. Sure, you've enjoyed yourself—why not? Every teenager needs a bit of a fling.'

'My fling lasted quite a while,' she frowned, 'until I found out about Father's troubles, last year. If only I'd known he was in debt! Why did he let me fritter money away? Why did he encourage me to travel?'

'He doted on you,' replied Cormac. 'He wanted you to experience the world and not resent the isolation of Cashel. It was important to him that you made a good marriage, too, so you had to meet the right people. And there was his pride, of course, in protecting the O'Connells from the taint of poverty.'

'We grew quite close before he died last month,' mused Caitlin. 'He was a loving man, under that coat of prickly armour—that's why I hate the way the newspapers have dragged his character through the mud.'

'And yours,' said Cormac grimly. 'They made you both out to be unfeeling: your father a drunkard who rejected his daughter; you a hard-hearted bitch! It's a pity they haven't been around to see the way you've worked over the last few weeks. You've hardly drawn breath. That would tell them something about your character,' he added loyally. 'I wish you'd sue the newspaper for libel; you'd have a rock solid case.'

Caitlin shrugged her slender shoulders and pushed back her straight, brown hair in an impatient gesture.

'I have too much on my plate; I don't think I could bear to go through anything else. In a way, it's my fault. I should have given all the reporters an interview and supplied a photograph. That would have satisfied them and they wouldn't have dug up a few isolated facts and strung them together in such a misrepresentative way. But it was awful, the way they descended on the house. How you stopped them from sailing to Brandon Island for Father's funeral, I don't know. I'll be eternally in your debt for the way you handled them.'

Her huge, brown, almond-shaped eyes met his and he winced at the pain within them.

'I made darn sure no one rented them a boat, that's all. At least the local people were on your side. Anyway, I'd do anything for you, Cait, you know that,' he said in a low tone.

She dropped her lashes and her long, thick brows met in one dark line as she chose to ignore the personal message.

'I know. You're a good manager, Cormac.' Aware of his hurt, and not sure how to keep his friendship without appearing to encourage him, she heaved a sigh, gave him a half-wave of apology and left quickly.

The last thing she needed at the moment was anything which touched her emotions; she was having enough trouble keeping them under control in public as it was. Instinctively she knew that, once she gave way to the powerful feelings simmering within her, she would never be the same cool, measured woman again.

The calm, remote manner protected her from the less appealing excesses of society life. Although she'd enjoyed the travel: cruising, skiing, house parties, luxurious living, and shopping in Paris and Italy, she'd frequently felt restless. In the last two years she'd hardly left Cashel at all, despite her father's urging.

Caitlin thought of something that Cormac had said: marriage. Of course! A wealthy husband, 'caught' on the jet-setting merry-go-round, would ensure that Cashel was never sold. Now she understood his eagerness to send her away. She'd believed that he didn't really want her around. If only he'd said! But Seamus O'Connell must have known that she'd fight such an idea.

None of the men she'd met had appealed to her in any other way than as amusing companions. The majority were too immoral for her taste, too—hence her assumed detachment. They'd come to realise that Caitlin simply didn't join in certain activities. It earned her the reputation of being wise and enigmatic, and saved her from unwelcome approaches.

'Cold-hearted Caitlin' was the tag they'd given her. And she was doing everything she could to live up to it, even now, at Cashel. If anyone ever suspected the seething passions of sorrow and suppressed, locked-in love, and made her emotions surface, she'd be diverted from the mammoth task of dragging herself out of debt.

Since her father's unexpected death, everything had been in a state of upheaval. Seamus had run Cashelkerry and the demesne like a benevolent despot, and her part had been to manage the house and act as his hostess. Now she realised that he'd been afraid to hand over the reins to her, because that would force him to admit that he'd lost his grip.

Caitlin paused in Cashel's vast hall, her eyes running over the faded damask paper which was peeling away at the broken cornices where the rain had penetrated. The antiquated central-heating pipes showed evidence of last year's sudden cracking, the walls stained from rusty water. It wasn't her father's fault that he'd been unable to manage things for the last year or so, she thought bitterly, catching a glimpse of her scowling face in the huge rococo mirror.

A slow, rueful smile curled her lips. Her society friends would hardly recognise her! Gone was the *soigné* chignon, the careful make-up, the couture elegance of her habitual slim-line suits and spindly stiletto heels. For practical reasons, since she had ceased to see visitors and spent all her time on the estate, she merely pulled her hair back from a centre parting and secured it with two combs, leaving the straight curtain of silken hair to fall to her shoulders. Yet, without make-up, dressed in a simple cap-sleeved ticking blouse whose deep scooped neck was edged with a flattering white lace, and a Ralph Lauren blue skirt which flared to her calves, she still looked stunningly beautiful.

Caitlin had the kind of face and natural grace which transcended anything she wore. The mysterious depths of her eyes, the natural blush in her cheeks and the perfectly curving lips had ensured her many suitors and a wonderful whirl of parties and invitations to exotic locations. After her father's reticence, the flattery had been pleasant.

It was a year ago that she had become aware of her father's troubles. Despite her urging, Seamus had refused to let her redecorate the run-down house. Finally, he'd told her why.

Jake Ferriter! Her eyes flashed dangerously. He'd been responsible for her father's decline—and Cashel's. He'd crippled the O'Connells financially, and perhaps emotionally. As her father had explained, she'd cringed at the despairing slump of his once proud figure. Apparently, they had never rightfully owned Cashelkerry!

Cursing Fate, and the Ferriter family in particular, Caitlin snatched an antique blue shawl from the hall-stand and flung it around her shoulders. The September sun would be sinking in the west by the time she returned.

She strode down the drive, the sad memories persisting. Her father had said their only possessions were the strip of useless bogland and a derelict farmhouse beyond the castle on Ferriter's Crag. Jake Ferriter, reported to be a mercenary American businessman, could have thrown them out of their home. Her father had fought a lengthy legal battle that cost every penny he had, pleading ownership by rights of three generations of tenancy. Then, strangely, Ferriter's solicitor had withdrawn the action.

Caitlin wished her father had told her earlier and not borne the burden alone. They'd never been very close; both of them had gone their separate and rather desperate ways when Caitlin's mother and brother were drowned in the dangerous straits between the beach and Brandon Island.

She had lost herself in the emotional anonymity of the select and protected group which enjoyed itself ceaselessly in the smart spots of the world; her father had taken comfort in whiskey. Their story wasn't unusual; the sea and alcohol had claimed many lives in this remote part of Southern Ireland.

Yet her father must have cared for her, to spare her the worry about Cashel until the danger of losing it was past. But the worry, the drink and the battle had broken him. His heart had been weakened by drink and stress.

Caitlin blinked furiously, trying not to recall the moment when she had burst into the study, full of delight because someone had booked up the long-house for a month's holiday. Since discovering their debts, she'd worked hard during her spare time to prepare the deserted group of houses by the beach for holiday lets, not expecting to let any this late in the season. The income wouldn't be much, but she was inordinately pleased with her efforts.

Her delight had turned to ashes at the sight of her father, slumped at his desk, the telephone buzzing in his lifeless hand.

Caitlin turned blindly into the lane, and her own hand reached out in a helpless gesture towards the profusion of wild flowers growing in the banks of the narrow road. She grasped a fistful of montbretia, the delicate orange trumpets poignantly reminding her of the day when she had plucked armfuls of wild flowers and sat as silent and still as a statue in the boat behind the funeral launch. On Brandon Island, out in the bay beyond White Strand beach, was little Brandon Church, where O'Connells and Ferriters had been buried for the last nine hundred years.

Now, she systematically shredded the bright orange petals. Her skin was stained with their juice and she didn't even notice that her distressed fingers spread dark stains on her skirt, too.

How tired she was of drawing on her inner strength! Sometimes she longed to lie late in bed and to be carefree again. Yet Caitlin knew how important it was that she kept a grip on herself. There were too many people on the estate relying on her for a livelihood; she couldn't wallow in misery at her plight.

If only people didn't interpret her control as callousness! She *hadn't* been the cause of Cashel's debts— not wittingly, anyhow. She groaned at the thought of all the money she'd spent, money which might have gone towards the upkeep of the house, or the legal fees. Her father, a great gambler at the best of times, had placed all his faith in his daughter marrying a millionaire.

Jake Ferriter, she thought, glaring sightlessly at the ground, you have destroyed my father and possibly Cashel itself. How on earth was she going to repay the debts?

A sound impinged on her mind. She looked up and cocked her head on one side, listening. Drowning the thin cries of piping plovers came the unusual throb of a powerful car. It was travelling very slowly, negotiating the sinuous bends of the lane. Caitlin ran over the possibilities, knowing that no one around here had an engine sounding remotely like a purring tiger!

It couldn't be the woman who had booked the longhouse, because she wasn't due till the next day. She frowned. Since the car had presumably passed through the gate announcing this was private land, it might be one of her boyfriends. Although her relationships with men were rather distant, her beauty made her a popular choice, and she was often photographed in exclusive restaurants on the arms of high-born young men. None of them had contacted her lately. Her mouth twisted. She wouldn't have thought that was from a sense of respect for her sorrow. Now the newspapers had torn her character to shreds and publicised her poverty, none of her male friends would want to be associated with her.

Caitlin had no desire to be the object of pity. Everyone she knew must have read that wretched article and would be aware that her father had died a drunken pauper. So who was coming this way at this time of day? Grimly she clambered up the steep earth bank, grabbing tufts of thick, heathery turf for support. She stood on the dry-stone wall, trying to see who it was. The car had turned on to another track, its engine growing fainter, and she stepped down in relief, deciding to sit on the wall for a while in the warm sunshine.

Her skirt spread out its deep blue folds over the lichen-covered stones, revealing a froth of lace petticoats above her golden-tanned legs. She kicked off her flat sandals and wriggled her feet in the lush grass. Wild bees, nesting in the wall, murmured sleepily, and she let her mind drift, tipping up her face to the sun's rays, listening to the sounds of the countryside. It had been a long time since she had found a space in her frantic life lately to do nothing but enjoy Cashelkerry's wild, natural beauty. She knew now why she always returned and never, ever, wanted to live anywhere else. She must keep Cashel!

From her vantage-point she could see a haze of red, where the wild fuchsia marked the many criss-crossing lanes. Fuchsia was a common hedge hereabouts, and a wonderfully exotic sight in late summer.

Then, somewhere in the depths of one of the lanes, the car could be heard again, reversing faster than she'd dare—and she knew every inch, every pot-hole. Suddenly the sound of the engine changed and the car was in sight; Parisian number-plates, which were all the rage, the coachwork a filthy red, but unutterably sleek, nevertheless, and driven by a man whose elegance surpassed even the beautiful, open-top car.

He stopped immediately below the wall where she was sitting and looked at her curiously, rather startled, she thought. He took in her bare feet, the country clothes with the smears of orange on the draped skirt, and Caitlin's hauntingly lovely face.

For her part, she eyed him suspiciously, recognising his air of vitality and wealth. His cuffs were starched and pure white, the equally blinding snow-white collar curving into a neck the colour of mahogany. An expensive tan, one which had been carefully cultivated by serious sunbathing. The navy suit was a fine summer weight and devastatingly tailored to a body devoid of fat, as if he ate well, but carefully, and spent time in a gym to preserve his much-loved body. She knew his sort. She'd spent some time with men like that. They made no demands on her because their emotions were purely on the surface. To a man, they were vain and selfish.

Her detailed scrutiny was interrupted.

'I'm trying to find Cashelkerry,' said the man in an accent she couldn't place.

But Caitlin was more interested in his destination than the way he spoke. Instantly alerted, her soft mouth tightened and she scanned the car for information about him. Her glance rested on an expensive camera, lying on top of a camera bag bulging with equipment. There was a cassette recorder on the seat too, a notebook, and a copy of the *Kerry Times*. She felt her breath come faster. His tools of the trade were those of a journalist, though she hadn't known any as flash as this before.

Caitlin's throat felt dry as a few facts fell into place. He must be from *Who's Where?*—the smart international society magazine whose pages were filled with scandal about the jet set. They'd rung her from Paris and tried to get an interview with her last week! She'd slammed the phone down on them. At the moment, of course, the man didn't know who she was. She'd have to be very wary, or he'd realise.

A faintly amused smile had lifted the corners of his mouth. It occurred to Caitlin that, from her slow response and rather startled expression, he thought she was simple-minded! Fine—she'd played that part before with reporters at the time of her father's funeral, very successfully. They'd never guessed her real identity, so intent had they been on interviewing a smart society beauty!

Her eyes widened and she blinked, trying to look perplexed.

He turned the engine off and the brief silence was filled with mocking choughs overhead. 'Cashelkerry,' he repeated slowly. 'That's where I'm heading.'

'Are ye now?' she said in mild interest, with a broadening of her soft Irish brogue.

He smiled patiently. 'Yes. Am I on the right road?'

'You could be. It all depends,' she answered, dead-pan.

A slight lift of his broad chest told her that he was slightly irritated. A man in a hurry, a man with a purpose. He wouldn't have time for bandying words.

Caitlin relaxed and put her heart into ridding herself of the unwelcome intrusion into her life.

'Depends on what?' he asked.

'On whether you're coming or going.'

'I said I was going there.'

Caitlin was pleased to see that his nostrils had flared and his jaw was jutting out assertively. Instead of regarding her with a rakish male admiration, he was now looking at her with a penetrating stare. She could see that he wasn't used to being thwarted.

'Oh.' Caitlin examined her big toe with great interest and bent down to flick off a small black ant.

'Am I on the right road?' he asked tightly.

She considered for a while. 'Sort of.'

It was all she could do to keep her face straight when he turned his dark head away and appeared to swear silently at the inoffensive bank opposite. Then his head swivelled around again and she was fixed with glittering green eyes, as hard and cold as the cruel sea near Brandon Island.

'If I drive up this lane, will I reach my destination?'

'No, not at all. If you had caterpillar tracks on your car, you'd reach the Atlantic. Since you haven't, you'd get stuck on White Strand. The beach is awful soft.'

'So it's not up the lane. Then which way do I go?' he asked with a grim patience.

'Up the lane,' she said innocently.

'But you said . . .' He lowered his voice and persevered in a quieter tone. 'You said I'd hit the beach.' He consulted a map with a ferocious frown. 'None of these roads match up with reality,' he muttered to himself. 'There are far more turnings than there ought to be.'

'It's true,' she admitted, enjoying the sight of a suave man out of his depth and floundering futilely. 'When we want to get anywhere quickly, we make a little road. Lots of ways, lots of choices.'

'Perhaps,' he said with an unnerving edge to his voice, 'you might tell me the choices.'

'I will that.' She settled herself more comfortably on the wall and stared at him, her sweetly ingenuous expression masking her rather malicious delight. She sounded more Irish than anyone could imagine!

He waited politely for several seconds for her to continue, and there was a dawning realisation on his face that she had no intention of doing so. Caitlin saw in fascination that his mouth had taken on a grim line and his biceps were spoiling the line of his suit as they tightened all the way down his arm to the bunched fist that lay along the dusty red paintwork.

The door was wrenched open as his fury broke, and Caitlin clung defensively to the stone wall, tensing uncertainly. For, when he swung his legs out and stood with a violent, angry movement, she saw that he was taller than Cormac, who was a bulky six foot, and, although his body was less densely packed with muscle, the way he moved menacingly towards her made her think of a powerful, hungry wolf. He had the air of a man who could handle himself in a fight and relished physical action. For the first time in her life, she was afraid of someone. Proud Caitlin O'Connell, who could repel unwelcome attentions and pestering hangers-on with a single icy stare, had met a man who believed himself to be superior to her. And that made her determined to prove him wrong.

However sophisticated, no hack sensation-seeking journalist was the equal of the O'Connells! They were Ireland's aristocracy, and the sooner this man knew that, the better. Then she remembered. For her own protection, she had to act like a fool. Hastily she lowered her lashes and pretended to be adjusting her neckline, which had slipped to expose a softly rounded golden shoulder.

'Are you intending to walk, now?' she asked as he stood glowering at her.

'No. Climb. It seems,' he bit, beginning to clamber up the bank, 'that I'm not going to get any sense out of you from a distance.'

A small frown creased her brow as she watched his progress. This was a wolf with a wounded leg. He hardly put his weight on it at all. She peered down at the inside of the car and saw that it was an automatic, so that the damaged leg wouldn't matter. His hands were close to her feet now, as he struggled up, and she pointedly swung her legs away, wishing that her many petticoats didn't rustle so alluringly.

His hard, unfriendly eyes flickered over the long bare shins, surrounded by scalloped white lace. Briefly his tongue moistened his lips, and then he was standing close to Caitlin, crowding her. She gazed in the opposite direction, uncomfortable with his intimidating manner.

'I think it's time you helped me,' he said harshly.

'Do you now?' she tossed in a lilting voice, slanting a look to see his reaction. It appeared he was clenching his teeth as hard as he could, in a slow, controlled fury. But the light in his eyes frightened her and she decided she'd gone far enough. Somehow she had to get rid of him. So he wanted help, did he? She would be very, very helpful. 'Let's see.' Caitlin thought deeply. 'There's a lot of turnings, so many ways you could go.'

'Just direct me,' he grated.

'Well, if you go up this road, you'll come to the lane to Murphy's place. He collects the milk around here. People take it to pick-up points on the road and...'

'Forget the milk collection. Get on with the directions.'

'Oh, yes. Then there's two little lanes either end of the Strand—that's the beach—and one before them that goes nowhere really, just over the peat bog. It used to lead to some homesteads, but they've been deserted, ever since the Emigrations.' She puckered up her face in thought. 'Now before that, but after Murphy's, is the turning to Smerwick Harbour and one to Ferriter's Crag.'

Caitlin paused, as his eyes flickered in some kind of recognition. However, he made no comment, just waited grimly, his arms folded across his big chest which had begun to move rapidly as his anger increased. She gabbled on, expecting him to give up any moment now.

'Well, of course, you don't want any of *those*.' She forced herself to remain innocently in place as his indrawn breath indicated he was coming to the end of his tether. 'Sure, it's a terrible place for getting muddled. The best thing is to turn around in the next gateway and go back to Dingle town. Cashelkerry is an awful difficult house to find.'

'Like hell I will!' he muttered. 'It can't be far. I have a reasonable sense of direction. If it wasn't for the fact that these roads twist and turn so much, doubling back on themselves, I'd make my own way. One last time, tell me how I get there, using old-fashioned words like "turn right", and "straight on", that sort of thing.'

'Ah, *that's* what you're wanting.'

The silence between them grew, and so did the tension. Caitlin quite admired his persistence and the way he was trying to control his anger.

He gave a sigh. 'Look. Tell me if the house is signposted or not. All I've seen for the last ten miles is a sign advertising bed and breakfast somewhere around here.'

Caitlin hid a smile. He was a fool to tangle with the Irish. Clever reporters before him had been driven mad with the confusion sown in their minds, not only by her, but the supportive local people, in the weeks following her father's death.

'A sign?' she asked brightly, clasping her hands in simulated fascination. 'Was that O'Sullivan's? Did it advertise bathrooms en suite?'

The man's teeth grated together alarmingly. '*No*! Hell, I should never have mentioned the damn sign and diverted your wandering mind. It's a miracle I've got as far as I have along this network of tracks. How on earth are people supposed to find their way without signposts?'

Caitlin's full, curving mouth swept into a slow smile, her lips arching like a drawn longbow. 'Sure, 'n why would we be needing a sign telling us what we already know?'

She'd gone too far. Her mischievous nature had made her go over the top with the play-acting. The man had gripped her shoulder with his huge hand, making her very aware of the delicate fragility of her bones and the power he could wield if he desired.

'That's enough,' he said, in a soft mutter filled with menace.

In those two words was carried a wealth of information. This was no kindly Irishman, to be gently diverted with laughter or a rueful glance. Nor was he like anyone else she'd ever met, not even the most blasé of the jet-setting crowd. He was hard as steel, through and through, utterly determined not to be beaten or fooled, never giving in, never taking the easy way out. He would go on and on until he landed on her doorstep, and would hang around until he realised that the simple country girl was really Caitlin O'Connell herself.

Her wary eyes had lifted to question his and her lips parted at the quality of intense masculinity that seared through the air between them, cutting her courage to ribbons. It was all to do with the eyes. They were the eyes of a man who knew all about women and their pretences, who found them occasionally amusing, occasionally exasperating, a man who knew how to remain dominant and persuade women to remain subservient to him.

The eyes had changed subtly. There was an unnerving sensuality in them; not that of a seductive lover, but a pillaging conqueror. She wasn't safe, that was for sure. He'd earned that hard, hewn face, the tough body, the inhumanly commanding eyes and the injured leg—earned them through bitter experience and cruel lessons that had never once defeated him.

It was no use trying to outface him. Her only defence lay in stupidity. Maybe if she didn't waver, he'd believe she was an imbecile and give up expecting sense from her. She could be as persistent as he could!

Caitlin lowered her eyes with some difficulty and picked a long piece of cotton grass, to chew yokel style. It was pulled from between her teeth in a swift movement that she didn't even see coming.

'I am not amused by your behaviour any more,' he said quietly. 'I am fully aware of the fondness of the Irish for intrigue and mischief-making, so stop pretending to be a gormless colleen. I've known for a while that you've been playing some kind of infantile game with me, and I find it infuriating.'

She was disappointed. She'd thought he'd swallowed her impersonation, hook, line and sinker. 'It's not a game,' she said, quietly morose. 'Not a game at all.'

'How sincere you sound,' he sneered. 'Stop lying and use your common sense—you've been found out. You have intelligent eyes in that beautiful face, however much you try to hide them.' His face bent close to hers and she felt the quick rush of his impatient breath on her skin. 'Give me directions, or so help me, I'll shake them out of you!'

Caitlin defiantly knocked his hand away and their eyes locked in battle. Perceptive he might be, but she was determined to get the better of him.

'Do you want to go by the Strand or would you prefer to go past the Standing Stones?' she enquired.

'Take care, pretty maid,' he growled. 'I want to go by the most direct route. The quickest way.'

He wanted directions, he'd get them! Caitlin took a deep breath, forcing herself to ignore his angry mouth. The more she stayed cool and unconcerned, the more likely it was that she'd come out the winner.

'Right you are, now. Go along the lane for about three minutes, or maybe two if you're driving fast, though at the rate you were going earlier, it may be five. Turn off at the milk churn if it's there, though it might not be, in which case...'

Caitlin gasped as she was suddenly lifted right off her feet by a pair of strong hands clamped under her armpits. She was terrified that they would both topple down the steep bank, and her slender body went rigid.

'You'll get in my car and you will show me,' he said, through clenched teeth. 'I've had a long journey and I'm tired.'

'Put me down,' she seethed.

'Not till you promise to take me to Cashelkerry,' he said remorselessly.

His grip tightened and she swung in the air a little, feeling quite ridiculous gazing down on him. He looked even more menacing, the way he was glaring up at her. She counted on the fact that he wouldn't be able to hold her up there for much longer, but he showed no sign of strain and had brought her closer to his body so that his eyes were in line with her breasts. Her nerve failed.

'All right,' she said reluctantly, wondering at the quickening of her breath. 'I'll show you the way to the house, though you'll be wasting your time. No one's in.'

He lowered her slowly to the ground and she was relieved when her bare toes sank into the welcoming turf. He'd begun to make his way down the bank and she started after him, but found that her skirt had snagged on a bramble. He sensed the fact that she had stopped; turned, watched her dragging at it impatiently, then reached up. He brushed her hands away and carefully, delicately, eased each thorn out of the material so that it didn't tear. His impossibly thick, dark lashes lifted momentarily as he released the last thorn, and Caitlin could have sworn that a spark had flashed through the short distance between their tensed bodies.

The sensuality of his mouth made every cord in her body vibrate with a bewildering weakness. But, as she reeled from the unexpected assault on her dormant senses, she discovered that all softness had been wiped from his face and in its place was anger, so swift and violent that she had the impression that he resented the brief loss of control and had no intention of letting a transient attraction for a stray woman rule his actions in any way whatsoever.

His eyes had narrowed to a hard agate. In a slightly contemptuous gesture, as if reinstating his position of mastery, he held out his hand to help her down the bank.

Angered by his behaviour, and thinking to take him down a peg or two, she spoke without thinking.

'Can't you manage? Do you need assistance?' she asked solicitously, stretching out her hand too, in a helpful gesture. Too late, she realised that her mockery had misfired: he'd think she was referring to his injured leg. Two bright spots of colour hit her cheekbones.

'Damn you!' he muttered. Abandoning her, he scrambled awkwardly down to the car. More slowly, Caitlin followed. He made no move to open the door, but sat glowering at the lane ahead. She walked around the car and slipped into the passenger seat, noting that he'd moved the camera and equipment into the back. Pity. She wouldn't be able to see what was written on the open pages of the notebook.

'Straight up the road,' she said quietly. The engine purred into life and the car moved cautiously over the uneven surface.

'Straight?' he queried sourly. 'On these bends? On this surface? Driving here is like riding on a neurotic duck's back.'

Caitlin smiled, despite herself, then gasped as a jolt rattled her teeth.

'Put your seat-belt on,' he snapped.

'This is a private road. Besides, no one round here bothers with those things. There isn't enough traffic to keep clicking yourself in and out. You can't be *that* bad a driver,' she added incautiously.

'You'll obey the law in my car,' he growled.

Caitlin gripped the seat as the car bounced over a pot-hole. 'Don't worry. There's no one to enforce it. We have our own laws in Kerry,' she said, trying to make out that they were all lawless and dangerous.

'Put it *on*!' he barked, reaching over for the belt.

As he did so, the low-slung Maserati lurched over the little humpbacked bridge that spanned Murphy's brook, and Caitlin's warm breast seemed to thrust itself into his curling fingers. He withdrew his hand as if he'd been scalded and switched all his attention to the road, while Caitlin hastily buckled the seat-belt, too late to prevent the unwanted contact and wishing she hadn't started this silly game. But there seemed no way to stop, and she wasn't prepared to let him win. She was behaving in a way she didn't really like, trapped by his appearance into lies and evasion.

'What do you want at Cashel?' she asked, taking the bull by the horns. If he answered honestly, she could tell him he was wasting his time. Perhaps it would have been better to do that in the first place!

'I have to pick up some keys there,' he said. 'I'm here on a month's holiday.'

Her gasp of astonishment made him throw her a puzzled look.

'No, you're not. You're not Miss Louella Seymour!' she accused. That was the name of the woman with the throaty voice who'd booked the cottage. 'Besides, she's arriving tomorrow!'

Her surprise was diverted by his incredibly white teeth and the genuine laughter erupting from his chest. He did look handsome when he did that, she mused.

'I am definitely not Louella.' He grinned, the laughter remaining in his voice. 'She's all woman and I, as you see, am all male. Every inch.'

Caitlin felt disturbed enough by the sensual way he said that to feel the need to stare ahead, to prevent instant hypnotism from his sultry eyes.

'She made the booking for me,' he went on. 'I was intending to stop in Cork for a night, but decided to drive over all in one day.'

The car slowed to a halt and Caitlin realised that she had been so intent on trying not to be affected by his considerable charm that she had missed the turning and they were at the head of White Strand.

'We've overshot the turning! Sorry,' she said apologetically, feeling a fool. 'I really didn't mean to misdirect you. We shouldn't be here at all. I was miles away.'

'I'm glad you were,' he said softly, and she looked at him quickly, wary of his intentions. But he wasn't interested in her, only the pure white sands. 'My,' he murmured. 'This is a wild and glorious place! Peopled by a wild and glorious people.'

Then he did look at her, and she trembled at the message in his eyes. It was a message that told her of potential danger, and she wished that she wasn't alone with this predatory, eminently virile stranger in such a remote place. The hairs on the back of her neck prickled into life as he turned off the engine, his compelling green eyes never leaving her face.

CHAPTER TWO

'YOU can reverse here and I'll show you where to go,' said Caitlin hastily.

'In a moment. I see no reason to waste the view.' He smiled gently and, with a wicked quirk of his mouth, turned his attention to the scene before them.

The curving half-moon of sand stretched invitingly between low, sea-girt headlands which arced on either side like the pincers of a crab. From each rocky point, rocks and small islands rose in craggy majesty from the blue-enamelled sea.

'What's that place?' he asked curiously, pointing to the forbidding black island across the Strait.

'Brandon Island.' Her almond eyes grew sad.

'And is it inhabited? I can see some buildings on it.'

'No one lives on it. There's a ruined church, rebuilt after the Danes sacked it in AD 800. Monks lived there once. That's the dome-shaped building you can see.' Her tone had become abrupt.

'Interesting. Tell me more.'

He'd turned to her again and Caitlin concentrated on the oystercatchers, scampering on the shoreline. But her emotions were in turmoil, stirred by memories, and what she saw was a terrifying image. A warm hand rested on her cold, trembling fingers. Expecting some kind of pass, her liquid eyes flashed a warning at him. But she saw only compassion in his face.

'What is it? What's the matter?' he asked very softly.

She closed her eyes, but the image persisted and so she squeezed them tightly together. He held on firmly to her hand and she gripped hard. It was a while before she was in control again, but he hadn't moved or made a sign to indicate that he was impatient with her unexpected behaviour.

'I'm sorry,' she whispered. 'I don't know why it should all hit me now. It never did at the time. Not like this.'

'Something upsetting? Why don't you tell me? It might help, whatever it is. Strangers can be easier to talk to than close family.'

'I have no close family,' she said in a low tone, then tried to hide her distress by changing the subject. 'Look, while you're here, you must never bathe off this beach, however tempting it looks.'

He frowned, not seeing the connection. 'I'm a superb swimmer,' he said, without seeming to boast.

'It doesn't matter how good you are,' she said earnestly. 'In certain tides, the Strait is lethal. It has claimed many lives.'

'Ah. Someone in your family?'

She nodded, and his comforting hand squeezed reassuringly.

'Recently?' he asked.

'Not really.' Suddenly the words flowed out unchecked. 'Eight years ago, when I was fourteen. I'd come down to the beach, to revise for my exams. Mother and my little brother Patrick were sailing over to the island to tend Grandpa's grave. The wind suddenly changed.' Her voice grew quieter and he leaned closer to hear. 'I watched them tip into the sea.'

Before he could speak, clear and tragic came the cry of a curlew calling plaintively, the note piercing Caitlin' heart with its melancholy. She gave a sob and tore herself away, flinging open the car door and racing blindly on to the beach.

He followed, as she knew he would. But, however sympathetic and nice he was turning out to be, she didn't want to share her distress, or to explain that it was the added stress of more recent events which had finally caused her to lose control.

Her feet plashed into the wet sand. Alarmed plovers took to their wings, filling the air with liquid notes, and then she was startling the braver oystercatchers too, till they rose in a soft whirr of black and white wings, flapping low over the glassy sea.

She was aware he'd stopped running in his slightly uneven gait. She sat down on the sand, glad not to force her shaking legs any further, and hugged her knees to her chest, rocking herself gently and waiting for the awful choking lump in her throat to disappear. Then, after a long while, she turned her head and saw that he was standing a decent distance away, patiently waiting. He was a thoughtful man. A rush of warmth towards him made her want to pour out all her troubles, a feeling so unusual that it made her brows meet in a frown of incomprehension.

She rose in a graceful movement and he came to meet her.

'Can I take you home?' he asked gently.

She struggled against the urge to lean on him for comfort, wondering why she should feel this way towards a stranger. Perhaps it was because he didn't know anything about her, didn't have a preconceived idea that she was cold and unemotional. But he was here for a month and she might have to face him again. She couldn't cry on his shoulder, however much she longed to.

'No. I'll make my own way. Thank you for being so understanding. Is it just the keys you wanted at Cashel? You see... I was going to the long-house, to put flowers in the rooms. I have a key. We can walk from here, if you don't have too much luggage.'

His face was filled with pleasure. 'Flowers? That's a very welcoming gesture.' He smiled as they began to stroll back. 'I only have a couple of bags. It would be nice to walk. So, you keep the cottage clean, do you? Does that mean you'll come in every day?'

Caitlin hesitated. Sooner or later he'd find out who she was, and yet despite his sensitive handling of her outburst she wasn't quite sure about him. Her recent lesson of caution had been cruelly learnt.

'Do you need a maid? You seem the kind of man who can look after himself,' she said lightly.

He laughed and thrust his hands in his pockets. 'I am known for my self-reliance. But I'd rather be tended by a beautiful woman.'

Her dark, wet-spiked lashes flickered in his direction. 'I'll bet,' she said drily.

He smiled with enormous charm. 'I hope I'll see you again,' he said. 'Even if you're not prepared to cook and clean for me!' His grin took the edge off that chauvinistic remark, as though he were mocking his own laziness. 'After all, I'll never get off the Cashelkerry estate without a guide through the little lanes.'

'I haven't proved too reliable so far,' she smiled apologetically.

'Who cares?' he shrugged. 'What fool would ever want to leave? It's magical. Like an enchanted world, with a ruined castle up there on the promontory, if I'm not mistaken.'

Caitlin's breath caught at his obvious pleasure. For a sophisticated man, he was certainly appreciative of wild surroundings. Perhaps he had a soft inner nature, just like her. He was shading his eyes and peering at the castle, further along, on the edge of a soaring cliff.

'And there's even a lovely peasant girl thrown in, for good measure,' he commented. 'It wouldn't surprise me to see you turning into a princess.'

'Silly!' Caitlin helped him to unload the car, shouldering the camera bag and taking the cassette recorder. His remarks were too near the truth! The 'peasant girl' happened to own the land he so admired. Or, rather, owned its debts.

They walked along the beach path to Smugglers' Cove, with its small jetty. Here was the only safe place for the currachs to sail from. He asked about the tiny tarred boats, tucked behind the storm wall, and she warned him again about the dangerous waters.

'Only locals know the sea around here, and sometimes they're caught out too,' she said soberly. 'The currachs might look like little black beetles, but they're very seaworthy. They ride the waves like a seagull and are much safer than ordinary boats.'

'What are they made from?' he asked in apparent fascination.

Caitlin liked him even more. He sounded genuinely interested. 'The frames are a light wood, and then pieces of canvas are sewn together and tarred. It's easy to repair them then—all you do is cut out the damaged bit and sew in a new piece.'

'Interesting. The old ways are often the most sensible. And they take outboard motors, by the looks of it.'

'Yes. They're kept in one of the barns at Cashel House.'

'So these belong to the occupant? Will I need permission to use one?'

She grabbed his arm, loath to think of such a vital and alive man drowning in the treacherous seas.

'Please don't ignore my warning!' she begged, her eyes wide with anxiety.

His face softened. 'Are you always this passionate?' he murmured, to her surprise.

'Passionate?'

'It's obvious that you feel things deeply.'

Confused, Caitlin drew herself away and walked on, the long-house thankfully in sight now. He said the most unexpected things! And no one had told her she was passionate before—just the opposite, in fact. Funny how differently people judged you, though this man had been one of the few to see her in tears. After all, she'd kept a stiff upper lip ever since that day when she'd seen the hungry waters claim her mother and Patrick.

'I think it must be the surroundings,' came the man's voice, close behind her. 'They clutch at your heart, don't they? Few could fail to be moved to passion by this view.'

He'd brought a smile to her face again and she glanced up at him gratefully with shining eyes. They had just crossed the little stream which ran deep in a gully from the valley, and which was overhung with mountain ash, arbutus and wild roses. Tangling through these young saplings were the drooping tears of crimson fuchsia. Beyond, where the valley opened, spread the glittering wet carpet of bogland and its yellow splashes of ragwort.

On the distant horizon rose softly rounded mountains, a pastel mist in the heat haze.

'I love it,' she said softly. 'Every inch. Each tuft and grain of sand. There's nothing in the world to compare with it.'

'No.' His eyes were alight with pleasure and a strange kind of elation that was increasing with every second. 'I have found it,' he said cryptically. 'I know what I've been looking for all these years.'

'It's only a simple cottage,' she said anxiously, and was surprised by his burst of laughter.

He caught her by the hands, and to her utter amazement whirled her around exuberantly till she was breathless.

'What . . .?' She was whisked around again. 'Stop it!'

He let her go and raised an eyebrow, as if surprised by his own actions.

'I'm sorry.' He looked almost embarrassed at her astonished face. 'It's a long time since...' A shadow passed over his face and Caitlin was puzzled even more by the twist of pain that touched his mouth for a fleeting moment and then was gone, before she could be certain. 'I'm pleased to be here,' he said abruptly. 'Delighted. I've been looking forward to this for a year.'

'Sounds as if you drive yourself too hard,' she said, hoping to hear something about him.

The tenseness of his body flowed away as he drew in a deep breath of the clean air, scented only with the sharp salt of the sea and delicate pollen. She followed his gaze to the low cottage walls and waited patiently while he raised an arm and felt the thickness of the thatch, weighted down with huge stones and a network of ropes against the winter gales.

'It used to be a croft,' she explained, worried that he was expecting too much. 'For a fisherman and his family. It's traditionally furnished, but it's probably not what you're used to.'

He took the giant iron key from her uncertain hand and threw her a smiling glance over his shoulder as he unlocked the plank door and stepped inside. 'It'll do fine,' he said, looking incongruous, striding around the whitewashed room in his city suit. Yet when he stood in front of the massive stone fireplace, his hands clasped behind his back, he looked comfortably at home.

'If it rains, you might need the fire to dry things,' she said hastily, finding his huge and brimming personality a little too much in the confined space. 'That's the turf basket beside you and bog oak the other side, with more in the outhouse. The stove works from turf, too. I hope you can manage.'

She had her doubts. Lighting the stove was something of an art form. Maybe she ought to stay and get it going for him.

'I've lit all kinds of fires in all parts of the world,' he said casually. His roving eyes rested momentarily on her. 'All kinds of fires.' Caitlin backed towards the door, unsure of the meaning of that. Something warm certainly nestled within her body. She hurriedly told herself it was the glow of friendship. 'You say that's turf?' he queried. 'I thought the fuel here was peat?'

Now she was on safer ground! 'It is. We call it turf, though. I'll leave you, then.'

'Wait!' He'd taken two strides and was detaining her with a friendly hand on her shoulder. 'Tell me your name. If I see you in the distance, I can hardly shout "Excuse me, woman who started out being evasive and downright difficult, and turned out to be someone I want to befriend,'' now can I?'

Caitlin giggled at the way he rattled off a summary of their meeting. Impulsively, she decided to trust him. He really was very nice and she *did* want to be his friend. She had a feeling that it would ease her troubles. He was the kind of man who would have a world full of wise and objective comments to make.

Somehow, meeting him had made her suddenly aware of her own loneliness: a loneliness of spirit, rather than anything else. There were few people of her own age nearby—even Cormac was thirty-five—though that hadn't bothered her before. After all, the stranger must be nearly thirty. Yet she felt more at ease with him, and his manner invited confidences, despite his rather intimidating appearance. She was sure there was a gentle, humane man beneath the sophistication. And her heart went out to anyone who appreciated Cashel scenery as much as she did!

'I've been evasive for a good reason,' she said, smiling up at him. His concerned expression and warm hand encouraged her. 'You see, I've been pestered by reporters—I'll tell you the story another day—and I thought you were one.' She sensed a slight change in him and searched his face anxiously. 'You aren't a reporter, are you?'

'No, I'm not.'

'I'm so glad! Why don't you come up to Cashel House for dinner? I can explain then.'

'You're inviting me to Cashel?' he said in a strangely choked voice.

'Yes, It's my home. That's part of my confession. You were nearer to the truth than you imagined when you said your peasant girl might change into a princess. Though the transformation isn't quite that grand! I'm just the owner of the demesne.'

His hand dropped suddenly from her shoulder and she tried to understand why he was so still and silent, so condemning. Surely he wasn't sorry that she was a landowner?

'You...' He seemed to be finding it difficult to say the next word. 'You...*own* Cashel House?'

'And Cashelkerry estate,' she said nervously. 'I did nothing to deserve it...' She floundered at his cynical laugh. Oh, hell! Had he read the condemning newspaper article? Would she have to go into long explanations to clear her name before he accepted her friendship? A feeling of intense disappointment swept over her. 'Why should you object to me being the owner?' she asked, dismay filling her eyes. He might not be an innocent tourist, after all. Reporters were perfectly capable of booking holiday homes to get nearer to their prey, and also capable of blatant lies.

'Can you think of a reason why I should?' he asked grimly.

'Maybe. Look, someone has to own land. I can hardly help my birthright.'

His eyes flashed at her, as hard as pure malachite.

She took a deep breath, her lip quivering at his hatred. 'My father owned it and his father before him,' she declared.

'Your name?' he grated through his teeth.

'Caitlin O'Connell,' she answered, her eyes wide and bewildered. 'You're *not* a reporter, are you?'

'No.' He swung on his heel and she was confronted by a massive back, the fine navy suiting rising with his slow, measured breathing. 'Well, if you'll excuse me, I'd like to heat some water for a bath. It's been a long day.'

Although this was said lightly, Caitlin knew he was trying to contain his feelings about something. For the life of her, she couldn't imagine what.

'Thank you for all your help, Caitlin,' he said smoothly. 'I think I'll be very comfortable.'

'What about dinner?' Her curiosity had been aroused. She had to satisfy it. He fascinated her with his mysterious manner.

'If you don't mind, I won't accept your kind invitation,' he answered politely, as if they were strangers again. 'I'll have a snack and an early night. Is the car safe where it is, or can I bring it closer?'

'It's safe.' She tried to hide her disappointment. Men didn't usually turn her down, and she wanted this one to like her. Still, it did indicate that he wasn't investigating her. She brightened up. There would be other opportunities for them to get to know each other over the next month. 'You can drive around to the top of the cove if you like.'

'I'll do that. I expect I'll see you around,' he said briskly, beginning to unpack his bag.

Sensing herself dismissed, Caitlin nodded and walked out, feeling uneasy. He didn't seem like a hungry newshound underneath that hard exterior she'd been confronted with initially, but he could be lying. How could she find out for sure?

The sun had almost dropped behind Ferriter's Crag and the sky was rippled with purple. She quickened her steps, wanting to be home in twilight, realising with a start that she had completely forgotten to ask him his name. That would be remedied the next day, she decided. She'd find out all about him: why he'd chosen Cashelkerry to stay, how he'd managed to take a whole month's holiday, what his job was . . .

That evening she invited Cormac to join her for dinner. But all the while she realised that she was wishing she sat opposite the stranger, with his vibrant zest for life, and she remembered with a warm glow the way he had whisked her around in an impromptu dance at the sheer delight in his surroundings. Cormac was too deferential. She didn't want to be treated like delicate china. Then she felt ashamed. Cormac had stuck with her father and herself through thick and thin. He was a man in a million.

When she went to bed, she hung out of the Georgian sash window and could just see a thin stream of pale blue smoke spiralling up in the black velvet sky. A sense of pleasure flowed through her, laced with the anticipation of excitement.

In the morning, Brigit reminded her of an appointment in Killarney with her solicitor. Brigit was one of the few staff she'd kept on and came in for a few hours a day, apart from Sunday. Caitlin dressed in one of her sleek suits and spent a frustrating day, wishing she was helping mysterious strangers to explore. Over the next few days she was kept busy with accountants and the revenue men, who made her realise what a serious state the demesne had fallen into. Cormac worked closely with her, but she felt even more remote from him than before, because she was making comparisons with the stranger all the time and knew that she had met someone who could take friendship into another dimension.

Several times, when she was checking through a pile of documents, her eyes had drifted to the smoke from the long-house, now rising vertically into the blue sky.

'Know anything about the man who's in there, Cait?' asked Cormac, seeing her inattention.

'I let him into the house. He didn't give out much information,' she answered casually. Odd how little he'd said. She had been the one who had confided, he'd kept quiet about himself, apart from one or two hints.

Cormac was chewing the end of his pencil thoughtfully. 'There've been rumours. He's very nosy. Takes his camera everywhere. He's been seen up at the castle photographing the house, and writing things in a notebook. I didn't like to tell you this, Caitlin, but I'm sure he's up to no good.'

'He said he wasn't a journalist,' she protested, worrying about the odd behaviour.

'The man could say anything,' snorted Cormac.

'I'll go and ask him what he's doing,' she said decisively.

'You shouldn't go to him. Ask him up here. See him on your own ground. It'll intimidate him, especially if you keep him waiting for a bit and then interview him in the library. You could put on your cool lady look.'

She smiled wryly. 'Is that what I have?'

Cormac bent his head. 'Yes. Shall I go and ask him?'

'Please.' She wanted to know for sure.

'While he's here, I could look through his stuff.'

'Cormac! You can't do that!'

'If he's lying, you need to know. Anyone that devious can't be treated with normal courtesy,' he said firmly.

Caitlin went to the window. In the distance, a small, dark figure was walking over White Strand. A flash of sunlight betrayed his binoculars. Of course, he could be an avid birdwatcher. Whatever his reason for being here, she needed to know. And she wanted to see him again.

'Just ask him if he'd like to come for coffee or something. I couldn't let you search his belongings. That would be wrong.'

'Some circumstances call for drastic measures,' frowned Cormac.

'Let me see what I can find out first,' she said.

'OK. But I'll hang around by the long-house in case you think he's a shady character. Send me word and keep him here long enough for me to have a look around.'

'Well ... only if I send word,' she said, not liking the idea. 'And whatever you do, don't disturb anything, will you? I'd be mortified if he knew we'd been snooping.'

'I'll go now,' he said, his face grim.

'Give me a chance to change,' she urged.

'What for?' he glared.

'Intimidation,' she said calmly.

But she wasn't calm when she raced up the stairs. Her heart beat unnaturally and it wasn't the effort of running. Part of her wanted to confront him on equal terms as a sophisticated and cool woman, part of her wanted to surprise him with the way she could look when she really tried.

The housekeeper announced that there was a man to see her and he wouldn't give his name. Caitlin had barely begun her make-up.

'Ask him to wait in the hall,' she said, hastily applying eye-shadow. When she finished, she swept up her hair in a smooth, elegant knot on the top of her head and swathed a silken, emerald scarf around it, letting the ends trail to the nape of her neck. The scarf matched the heavy linen suit, which swerved in dramatically at her waist and flared into a feminine peplum. She pushed her feet into a pair of smart, high-heeled shoes and checked her reflection with satisfaction.

She hadn't lost her touch. She looked good. He was bound to be impressed, she thought, without vanity, and that would make her job easier. Without thinking, she crossed her fingers, hoping that he was only a tourist.

On the landing, she took a few calming breaths and strolled casually to the top of the wide staircase. His back was to her. He stood on the huge black and white chequered slabs, his hands in his pockets. Today he was dressed in a casual cream shirt, rolled up to the elbows, and a pair of dark gold trousers. As she began to descend, he turned slowly, with the same expression he'd worn when she'd annoyed him the first time they'd met.

She lifted her chin proudly and placed a pleasant smile on her face.

'How nice to see you,' she said, reaching the bottom of the stairs.

'You sent for me,' he pointed out grimly.

Her action sounded unpleasantly imperious, the way he described it. She hoped Cormac hadn't been too high-handed.

'What exactly did Cormac say,' she asked cautiously.

'That Caitlin O'Connell was expecting me at Cashel House in the next ten minutes.'

'Oh!' That didn't sound like Cormac. 'I'm sorry I've kept you waiting. I hope you weren't bored.'

'Not at all.' He gave a secret smile that excluded her. 'I've been looking around. Quite a place, is Cashel.'

His expression alarmed her. Was that polite interest in his voice, or intrusive nosiness? Was that brain of his—which she could almost see whirring away—mentally noting every detail of the dilapidation, and contrasting that with her obviously expensive suit? Caitlin cursed herself for overdressing. If he was a reporter, she thought grimly, she'd played right into his hands.

'We'll go into the library,' she said coldly.

With a mocking look, he opened the massive double doors and she walked slowly to the end of the long mahogany table, surprised that he didn't comment on the room. It was the pride of the O'Connells—although most of the books had once belonged to the Ferriters. There were many priceless volumes there, especially those in featherwork-tooled leather, some which she might now have to sell in order to keep the house going. She surveyed him from one end of the gleaming table, resplendent with Kinsale silver displaying the O'Connell armorial bearings. That at least was theirs. The Waterford glass chandelier caught the light from the floor-length windows and cast a kaleidoscope of dancing colours on to the bookcases. Caitlin sat down in a fluid movement. The man's eyes were absorbing it all.

'I wanted to talk to you about something,' she began. Illogically, she wanted him to comment on something else—the way she looked—but not by a flicker of his eyes had he shown surprise or pleasure, and her disappointment hit her forcibly, adding to her anger. 'I've ordered tea. I hope you'll have some. Please sit down.' She indicated the seat at the far end of the table, but he ignored it and wandered over to a side window with its panelled window-seat, looking out over the lush, green fields scattered with black-face sheep.

'How good is the grazing?' he shot.

'What?'

'I asked about the quality of the grazing.'

His snapped tone, half irritated, had annoyed her. 'I asked you here to question you,' she said coldly, beginning to think that Cormac and the rumourmongers were correct. They were both silent as Brigit brought in the tea.

'Put it down here, please,' he ordered.

Brigit responded to his tone of natural authority and began to take the tray over to him.

'Brigit! Bring it here!' she cried, glaring at him.

To her amazement, he strode over, took the tray away, placed it on the side-table near the window, where he'd indicated, and then took the bemused housekeeper by the arm and gently helped her out. Caitlin's mouth fell open at his nerve.

They were playing some kind of power game that she had already begun to lose. It was a pity she'd listened to Cormac and started acting like the Lady of Cashel. She ought to march over and take the tray from him, but that would be petty. How could she regain the upper hand? Caitlin fell back on the tested and successful frostiness for which she was famed.

'I'm not quite sure what you're trying to achieve,' she said, in a tone of bored disinterest, 'but please remember you are a guest in my house. You have changed from a rather thoughtful man into a rude, high-handed one.'

'You've changed, too,' he said. 'You're not the girl I met in the lane any more.'

Flushing at the regret in his voice, and sorry that he wasn't the kind of man who could cope with an inde-

pendent-looking woman after all, she tipped up her head
proudly.

'I didn't think you'd even noticed,' she commented.

'Of course I did. You made sure I'd know the difference,' he said quietly.

She groaned inwardly. 'I wasn't trying to... I mean,
I didn't intend to assert my position, or anything, I...'

'Milk?' he asked smoothly.

She nodded dumbly. This was going wrong. She rose
and came over to the window, taking the cup from him
with a brief thanks.

'Please understand that I have to be careful who I let
on to my land. You've caused a lot of talk with your
behaviour. I gather you spend a good deal of time poking
about and taking notes. No one around here likes in-
vestigators, be they journalists, the revenue men, or potential property developers. The people here are
protective of me and don't want snoopers. That's why
you're here, so you can clear things up.'

'By people, do you mean the jealous red-headed
giant?' His eyes glinted at her over the rim of his cup.

'Cormac couldn't possibly be jealous. And he's not a
giant. I don't think he's as tall as you. You're just as
muscular, and your shoulders are broader. It's...' She
looked down, confused, aware that he had become
cynical at the way her words were betraying her.

'Who is he? What does he do?'

'Cormac Kelly is my estate manager.'

'I've seen him around. I wondered what his role was
in your life.'

'Why are you being so unfriendly?' she asked quietly.
'What are you doing in such a remote part of the world?'

'Research.'

Relief flooded through her as all the clues slotted into place. Why on earth hadn't she thought of that? The notebook, the deep feeling about his surroundings—he was a writer! She beamed and relaxed completely. 'Now I understand. I wish you'd said. We would respect your privacy, you know. We appreciate writers.'

He regarded her with a calculating eye. 'You won't turn Cormac on me if I explore?'

Caitlin laughed happily. 'No! But . . . I would like you to have dinner. And if you like, I can show you around the estate. I'd love to. I need a break from endless meetings with men with only one thing in mind.' Her eyes twinkled at his raised eyebrow. She was thinking of accountants and solicitors and the bank manager; it was evident that he was imagining boyfriends! Perversity and pride prevented her from correcting his impression entirely truthfully. 'Money! All they think of is money. I'm sick of it. Please say you'll let me be your guide.'

He put his cup down and took hers away too, then seemed to be struggling with the desire to kiss her. Caitlin's heart leapt erratically with anticipation. His lashes dropped to cover the yearning in his eyes, and she felt a surge of disappointment.

'Why don't you?' she said breathlessly.

His lashes lifted again, briefly scanning her face. 'Let you be my guide around the estate, or around your mouth?' he asked bluntly.

She swallowed at her temerity. 'Neither of those possibilities is exactly world-shattering,' she answered as casually as possible.

A kiss was nothing nowadays, she told herself. She'd had plenty without them meaning anything. Except, if he touched his lips to hers, she believed she'd experience something special.

'I admire your disregard for my lips. Thank you for the offer, however little it means to you. I would rather not,' he replied in a low tone. 'But I'd like a guide around Cashelkerry. It would be very helpful for my research. May I see the house, too?'

Caitlin didn't know what to make of him. He *had* wanted to kiss her. It seemed extraordinary that he should pass up the chance! Now he had refused, her eyes kept going to his sensual mouth, willing him to feel the same way she did.

'Of course you can see the house. But I can't wander the fields like this. I'd better change,' she said.

'Oh, not now,' he dismissed. 'I have some papers to look at. I'll come tomorrow at nine-thirty.'

Caitlin felt slightly irritated. He was always managing things his way, not hers. And if he left now he'd find Cormac still outside the long-house!

'Stop for lunch and do your papers afterwards. And for heaven's sake, tell me your name! I can't keep thinking of you as "The Stranger"!'

'Thank you, no. I never put off what has to be done,' he said, his eyes serious. 'And forgive me, but I would prefer not to give you my name. You'll know soon, and I can promise you that I won't be a stranger then.'

'You're that famous?' she asked, impressed. He seemed very confident that she would have read one of his books, or heard of him in some way. 'I'd know your name, if you said it?'

He looked embarrassed. 'Yes,' he muttered. 'You'd know my name.'

Before she could stop him, he had spun on his heel and hurried away, as if something was troubling him. Caitlin was even more fatally intrigued than before.

CHAPTER THREE

THE next morning, Caitlin was preparing a picnic in the big family kitchen when the postmistress popped in for a cup of tea and a gossip. Hoping to keep her rendezvous with the stranger private, Caitlin fetched two mugs and tried to divert Mrs Murphy by asking about her family, but the woman got straight to the point.

'Is the new man in the long-house from England, then?' she asked, sipping the strong brew.

Caitlin's hand stopped buttering rolls. It was an interesting question. 'Do you know, I'm not sure! He has an odd kind of accent, one I've never heard before. How did you know about him, anyway?' she twinkled up at the postmistress, whose capacity for detective work was unsurpassed.

'Sure, it was such a lovely morning, I decided to drive along that way. And I was treated to the sight of the man, working away at his keep fit.'

'His what?' laughed Caitlin.

'Doing those press-up things, like he was training for the Olympics, he was. Stripped to the waist, too, and if I wasn't married to Murphy all these years I'd be down there courting him. He has a fine body, Caitlin O'Connell, I thought you ought to know!'

'Thank you, Mrs Murphy,' she said, repressing a smile.

'Off out with a friend?' asked Mrs Murphy, assessing the quantity of food Caitlin was packing into the wicker basket.

51

'Mr Keep Fit himself.' Caitlin knew it was hopeless keeping the information from her. 'Actually, he's a writer, looking for local colour.'

'Couldn't get better than Cashelkerry. Or the roses in your cheeks.' She laughed at Caitlin's blush which went right down to the V of her open-necked red shirt which she'd belted over a pair of old jeans. 'I remember you when you were an impulsive, affectionate little girl. Suit a writer, someone like that.'

'Stop matchmaking!' laughed Caitlin. 'Times have changed, Mrs Murphy. I'm not like that any longer. Nor do I wish to suit any man at the moment.'

'He's rich, so they say. Runs a costly car. You need a man with money.'

'I'm beginning to think you're right.' Caitlin gave a sigh, hating to be reminded of her horrendous debts.

To Caitlin's embarrassment, the open doorway to the hall was suddenly filled with the stranger's bulk. Her eyes darted to his feet, expecting him to be wearing trainers because of the way he'd crept up so silently, but he wore brogues. Either her hearing was faulty, or he'd purposely tiptoed from the front door.

The idea made her frown till her straight brows made a long, dark line. He had heard the remarks, judging by his hostile expression, and didn't like being the subject of gossip. Darn! Now it would prove difficult to get him chatting about himself, and she'd lain awake for quite a while the previous night, fascinated by his reticence.

'Hello,' she said warily. 'Who let you in?'

'No one.' His face had become impassive, though he seemed riveted by her red shirt. 'The door was ajar and I heard voices here.'

'Meet our postmistress, Mrs Murphy,' said Caitlin, still wondering how he'd got in. She was sure the door had been closed. And how long had he been listening?

'So you're the writer.' The older woman looked as if she was about to grill him, and Caitlin wanted to do that—slowly and tactfully! An assault now would make him clam right up.

'We have to go now,' she said quickly, handing him the basket and hurrying to the back door pointedly.

He nodded curtly at Mrs Murphy and followed Caitlin out, a feeling of tension emanating from him. She kept her eyes down as she stopped by the Land Rover, but could see that his hands were clenched. They were remarkably tanned, as if he'd worked outdoors all his life, though that didn't fit with his immaculate appearance when he'd first arrived. And now, she thought, sneaking a look at him from beneath her lashes, even though he wore a checked shirt and green cords, they were well-cut and hardly worn, as though he'd bought them specially for this holiday.

'How deeply the women assess a man around here, to be sure!' he murmured.

Her startled eyes met his, and she bridled at the mockery she saw.

'If you're wondering,' he continued, 'I paid quite a lot of money for my clothes. French. The label's in here somewhere.'

'Stop that!' she said, aghast, as he began to shrug the shirt out of his waistband.

He gave a faint smile. 'I wanted you to know that they were in keeping with my wealthy image. I'd make a good catch.'

Caitlin was embarrassed. 'Look, you mustn't take any notice of Mrs Murphy, she——'

'Oh, I don't. The question is, Caitlin,' he said sternly, 'do you?'

'No one takes any notice of gossip. She's harmless. It's very isolated out here and she loves it when new people come. Gossip is a release from loneliness,' she defended, not answering his question. He couldn't really believe that she looked on him as a possible husband! It was too ridiculous.

'It's intrusive,' he snapped. 'Before we go anywhere, I'd better make my position clear, so no one has any ideas about matchmaking. I'm not interested in marriage. My work is my passion. You wouldn't understand that, having spent your life flirting around the world and wasting your time generally.'

Caitlin's eyes blazed. So he *had* read that darn article! 'Now you're believing in gossip!'

'Isn't it true?' he challenged.

'I didn't flirt,' she said vehemently.

'But you concede that you wasted your life,' he said.

'I'm entitled to a bit of fun in my youth, aren't I?'

'Not if your father can't afford it,' he said tightly.

'I didn't know! I had no idea...'

'Why do you think that was, Caitlin?' he asked, his eyes opaque. 'Why didn't he confide in you?'

Her full mouth trembled. 'Why are you doing this to me?' she cried in despair. 'What right do you have to persecute me like this?'

'None,' he said surprisingly. 'Only a desire to find out what kind of person you really are, to know whether you are as shallow as you sometimes appear, or if there are depths behind those beautiful eyes.'

He'd done it again. He'd disturbed her senses, muddled her emotions and brought them to the surface. Although she ought to hate him for his rudeness and insolence, she found that her greatest feeling was that he had flattered her in an odd way. In the silence that had fallen, swallows chattered shrilly on the telephone wires above them, perching like little notes of music as they contemplated their flight to the tropics.

He followed her gaze. 'They're leaving Cashelkerry,' he murmured. 'All summer they've been here. How can they leave this place?'

Bewildered by the strength of feeling in his tone, she fought down an ominous feeling of foreboding. 'You confuse me,' she whispered.

He gave a crooked smile and touched her arm in an apologetic gesture.

'Good. You must forgive me, Caitlin,' he said in a voice as liquid as honey. 'It's the way I am. Part of my training is to dig deep into people and strip away the veneer. Sometimes I get carried away. With you,' his fingers lightly caressed her crimson sleeve and then dropped away, 'with you I get carried away more frequently than I should. It's all due to that Irish magic of yours. You're elusiveness is fascinating.'

'My elusiveness?' She frowned.

'Yes. Now you see it, now you don't,' he replied cryptically.

'I don't understand.' Writers were extraordinary people! He certainly knew how to ruffle up her calm exterior.

'Neither do I,' he sighed. 'Perhaps after we've spent a little time together we might understand a little better.'

She eyed him uncertainly. 'I don't know that I want to spend the day with you if you're going to make personal remarks all the time.'

Caitlin was dazzled by his disarming grin and weakened by the way his eyes crinkled at the corners. He was a devastatingly handsome man, she thought hazily. If only he didn't know that!

'I'll put a curb on my more intimate thoughts,' he murmured wickedly. 'Or at least, I'll try not to make you aware of them. And I'll put off delving into your mysterious soul. But...you know I have an ulterior motive for going around with you today.'

Caution filled her face. 'Ulterior?'

'Mmm. Research. Remember? You won't take flight if I fling questions at you, will you?'

'Oh! No, I love talking about Cashelkerry and its history.'

'Yes,' he said quietly. 'I'm particularly interested in that.'

'Well, let's get going, shall we?' she asked cheerfully. 'I thought I'd show you the land and we'd have a picnic. We'll start off in the Land Rover, but there'll still be a bit of walking, if that's all right,' she finished doubtfully, wondering about his leg.

'That sounds fine,' he said politely.

'Yes. But...you'll tell me if you're tired——'

'I think my stamina will surpass yours,' he said wryly.

'I was only thinking...well, you seem to have a slight problem with...your...um...injury.' Now it was out and he had to answer.

'It's nothing. Sometimes it's worse than others.'

Despite the fact that the shutters had come down over his face, wiping away the pleasant charm, she persevered, curious to know the trouble. 'How did you hurt it? Will it improve?'

He cleared his throat. 'An accident. Do you have a map of the estate? It would help if I could orientate myself.'

'Here, in the truck.' They climbed in and she pointed to the glove box. He sat in silence, absorbed, occasionally looking up as if to get his bearings. She drove him to the plantation, answering dozens of questions. He seemed interested in everything; whether the flat field behind the house ever became waterlogged, whether there were grouse on the hills, if there were mountain hares and plenty of rabbits. All the time, he gave the impression of being distanced from her, almost reserved, and she began to bristle a little at his impersonal manner and tried to accept that she was merely a source of information to him at the moment and he wasn't seeing her as a person at all.

That didn't help. She was far too aware of him herself. And the incident with the dog increased that awareness.

As they jolted over a pot-holed lane that ran through a luxuriant, uncut meadow, Murphy's dog suddenly appeared, barking furiously and running alongside the vehicle.

They both began to laugh; it was obvious that the old sheep-dog was trying to herd the Land Rover into some kind of order.

'Poor Danny!' laughed Caitlin. 'He's retired now and misses work. He's fantasising that we're a flock of sheep.'

'He has quite a turn of speed. Slow down a minute.'

To her astonishment, he jumped out of the moving vehicle, judging his landing perfectly, then he opened his arms to the dog and began to fondle it affectionately.

She drew to a halt and looked back, puzzling over the dark head buried in Danny's shaggy coat, and surprised by the gentle and experienced way that he persuaded Danny to sit and stay.

'Drive on,' he said quietly when he returned to his seat. He looked back, watching the mournful dog until they turned a corner. 'I had a dog like that once,' he explained, at her questioning look.

'Once?'

'He pined and died,' he muttered.

'Oh, I'm so sorry,' she said in compassion, seeing how much the incident had affected him. 'That's awful. Look, while you're here, I'm sure Mr Murphy would let you take Danny for walks—or rather go with Danny on *his* walks. Collies are independent dogs, not used to leads, as you probably know. Well, they are out here. Maybe your dog was different, being in a town.'

'Thank you, Caitlin,' he said softly, with a warmth that made her spine tingle. When he was nice, he was very, very nice. Too nice for her own good.

'Why...?' She bit her lip, wondering if she ought to go on, but her curiosity burned. 'Why should he pine? Did you leave him in kennels?'

His mouth tightened. 'No. I was away from him for a long time.'

Her brow creased. 'Couldn't you——?'

'No!' he snapped. 'My absence was unavoidable. Leave it. I don't want to talk about it.'

She slowed the vehicle and switched off the engine. He felt terribly guilty about causing the death of his dog, by putting his business interests first, thought Caitlin. She wondered if he'd been in hospital after a car accident. By the end of the day, she wanted to know everything about him. He was the most interesting man she'd ever met.

'I'm awfully sorry,' she said, impulsively turning and clutching his arm. His eyes swivelled to hers and she was shocked by the pain there. How odd, that this hard and controlled man should weaken at the loss of his dog! So he had a soft heart, and she wasn't the only one who had covered up a sensitive nature with a veneer of indifference!

'Don't look at me like that, Caitlin,' he said in a choked voice.

Suddenly she found that her heart was thudding unnaturally and his face had grown still. Beneath her fingers, his muscles had tightened and she knew that his whole body was tensing. Her face had softened as she leaned towards him, eager to be forgiven.

His eyebrows met in a V over his nose, and cynical lines appeared around his mouth. Then his head snapped back and he heaved a huge sigh of exasperation.

'For heaven's sake, drive,' he growled.

She stared, then, as he drew further into himself and ignored her, she recognised that his anger was not directed at her, but himself. He was afraid of his own softness, she thought with an inner smile. He'd been upset and looked to her for comfort, and now was trying to cover up his lapse. As they moved away, her mouth twisted wryly. It was just as well he didn't know what her reactions had been when she'd glimpsed his tender nature. For she knew that the rush of warmth and affection within her had been supplanted by a more dangerous sensation.

His withdrawal had been a great disappointment. For a moment, Caitlin had thought they were more than physically close. And she knew that she had wanted him to take her in his arms, to kiss her with that strong, masculine mouth, to murmur that he needed her... Caitlin drew in her breath deeply. He was completely unaware of her, yet she still tingled. All her senses were alert and focused on him.

She stole a surreptitious glance in his direction. There was a brooding quality about him, as if he too was confused at the turn of events. Caitlin believed that he rarely let people glimpse this gentler side, that he always tried to stay detached.

'Stop here,' he ordered suddenly.

There was a harsh note in his voice, as if to instil in her the realisation that he was back in control. Automatically, in response to his command, as if born to obey his tone of authority, she put pressure on the brakes and he jumped out again.

For all her feelings about him, Caitlin disliked her own reaction. Men didn't order her around, they were more than willing to fall in with her wishes. Slightly irritated, she flicked back her long fall of hair and followed. Writers might be preoccupied when researching, and he might be controlling his emotions, but nevertheless he could have asked politely!

They were at the foot of the rising land which led to Ferriter's Crag and the ruined castle, but he wasn't interested in that at the moment. He was examining the grasses and scanning the bracken along the lower slopes. Then he bent down and stared at something intently.

'What is it?' she asked.

'Deer,' he answered, absently, pushing at the dry droppings with his foot. 'Many here?'

'Cormac says there's a small herd of fallow deer in the old oak wood. I've seen the odd one or two, but I'm surprised they venture out this far.'

'I imagine they were after the young saplings over there.' He indicated an isolated group of trees and then scanned the hill above them, its slopes patterned by low crumbling walls. 'Plenty of cover.'

'Well, we didn't build those walls to hide behind and shoot innocent deer,' she said quickly. 'They're incredibly old—marking the ancient field system.'

'Don't get me wrong. I would never kill animals for sport, only food. How old is the castle?'

It topped Ferriter's Crag, a romantic, lichen-covered ruin silhouetted dramatically against the sky, its walls invaded now by thorn trees, twisted into arthritic shapes by the fierce Atlantic gales.

'It was built in the thirteenth century, right inside an Iron Age fort. Sir Walter Raleigh's men sacked it.' She paused at the gleam in his eyes and barely suppressed excitement which had brought his stony face to life. His interest made her feel happy again. 'The family who once owned our land were called Ferriter and were descended from a local chieftain. Are you interested in the story?'

'Oh, yes, I'm interested,' he murmured.

'The Ferriters were English, descended from the Normans. They were given Cashelkerry as swordland by Raleigh. The most famous of them was Piaras Ferriter, born in sixteen hundred. But he fell in love with the Irish people and sided with them against his old masters. That's what happens to most people who come here aconquering.'

'Oh?' He sounded disbelieving.

Caitlin smiled. 'It's true. In County Kerry, we know that no one has ever had a victory over the Irish people. They become absorbed into our culture instead. The saying goes that all would-be victors find themselves gloriously lost in the arms of our women.' She slanted an amused glance at him, to find he wasn't amused at all, but that his mouth had twisted sardonically.

'Very subtle. Such a saving on blood. So Ferriter lived happily ever after, in the arms of an Irish colleen?'

She sighed. 'No. He was hanged in Killarney by the Cromwellians.'

'It sounds as if he would have been wiser if he'd spurned the seductive women and kept his life and self-respect by sticking to his original job.'

'That's very unromantic of you!' she declared.

'But wise,' he said sardonically. 'Thank you for telling me the story. It's a lesson to be remembered, I think, if *you're* anything like the women around here.'

A quiver ran through her when he eyed her thoughtfully, and she bristled in anger at his male arrogance.

'I'm not sure I like you,' she said haughtily.

'Thank heaven for that,' he answered with feeling, making her flinch inside. He might be scared that she was after him, but he didn't have to be that blunt! She contemplated telling him that the tour was over, but that would look as if she'd been offended, and she didn't want to give that impression. He might think he mattered to her. She assumed a cold look of indifference instead. He flicked a sour glance at her. 'Let's get back to the research. Is that when the O'Connells took over?'

'No,' she said slowly, hoping he wasn't going to probe too deeply. 'The land lay derelict for a while and then the Ferriters got it back when the English left.'

'Where exactly do the O'Connells fit in? How did they come to lord it over the area?'

A faint flush of irritation coloured her skin at his tone. 'I don't know what you mean by "lord". They're an old family too. They were seneschals of the Princes of Kerry and owned the land over there.' She waved a vague hand at the rust-coloured bogland, realising an investigative man like him would now want to know how Cashel had been lost by the Ferriters and ended up in O'Connell hands. 'Shall we climb up?' she suggested, beginning to walk on in the hope of diverting him. 'There's a wonderful view to the beach.'

Fortunately, by the time they had completed the stiff climb, he had forgotten about ownership of land and was studying the sheer cliff-face below them. He lay on his stomach and edged over, looking right down, apparently without any fear of heights.

'This is a running tide, isn't it?' he yelled back at her, over the sea breeze and the roar of Atlantic rollers.

'What's that?' Caitlin was surprised at his knowledge, though she supposed men in his profession picked up all sorts of scraps of information.

'An incoming tide. Is the beach always exposed?'

'Yes, you can always walk around to Smugglers' Cove from here. Father was thinking of keeping a little boat on the beach, but never got around to it.'

'The bay is safe?'

She peered down at the rocks glistening with the brilliance of a gem. They edged the broad bay of pure untrodden sand, washed clean and flat by the Atlantic.

'If you can negotiate the breakers, yes, it's fine. We swim off here. The beach shelves so gently that there's always surf, and sometimes we take a board out and pretend it's Bondi Beach.'

He nodded in satisfaction and stood up, his eyes darting everywhere. Somehow he looked remote and harsh, with gannets screaming overhead and plummeting down the cliff behind him, and Caitlin shivered as ice travelled up her spine. Something was wrong. He was too calculating. She could almost see his brain whirring, processing information. He had the look of... Her stomach churned. It was as if he was assessing the land's value. Like a property agent.

'The grazing looks good.'

'What—what kind of book are you writing?' she asked suspiciously. He'd given the fields an unpleasantly proprietorial nod of approval.

'Book?' he queried with a sinister smile. Then he laughed at her worried face and bent to sift handfuls of soil through his fingers, apparently fascinated by its texture.

Trembling, she turned and stumbled back to the Land Rover, waiting for him and wondering what to do. An outright question wasn't going to get her far, he'd already tried to fool her with the idea that he was researching. All her instincts told her that wasn't true. He was playing with her, rather like the way she had played with him in trying to prevent him from reaching Cashel House. Was he being spiteful, then? Showing her what it was like to be fooled? If so, he was a mean kind of man, narrow and unforgiving!

He swung into the Land Rover arrogantly, as if she was driving him on a Grand Tour of his estate. Perhaps, she thought gloomily, she was. Perhaps the revenue men had tipped off a friend to look the land over, before they forced her to put Cashelkerry on the market. They'd already indicated that she would have fifty per cent of its value to pay in death duties.

In her agitation, she came to a decision. Sneaky or not, she'd do as Cormac had suggested.

'I have to speak to my manager,' she said shakily, starting up the engine. 'He's checking the timber in the plantation. We'll go that way to the lake. I'm sure,' she said a little sarcastically, 'you wouldn't want to miss the lake and the river, would you?'

'Very kind,' he murmured, and Caitlin could have hit him.

She drove to the forest in grim silence, leaping out and dashing over to Cormac, who had finished and was striding back to Cashel. She had a quick word with him and marched back in satisfaction. While she was keeping Mr Mystery busy, Cormac would make a careful search of the long-house and then they could both confront him with any evidence of underhand dealing.

'Your manager was hanging around the long-house yesterday. Is this part of the interest you all show in strangers?' he asked mildly.

Caitlin flinched. She'd quite forgotten! Poor Cormac, she hoped he'd dealt with the situation tactfully—though, judging by his earlier abrupt invitation on Caitlin's behalf, she doubted that!

'Cormac has work to do all over the estate,' she said firmly.

'Hmm. You'd better tell him I'm allergic to any invasion of my privacy.'

'I'll do that,' she answered, wondering why the two men had taken such an obvious dislike to each other.

And then she fell silent, absorbed by the scene before her. The lake was beautiful. She parked and they walked down to its edge. As upset as she was, Caitlin still felt more serene, just standing by its dark waters, which perfectly mirrored the huge oaks on the far shore.

'Plenty of fish in here?'

She glared at the question. If she didn't need to keep him busy, she would have stopped this farce. For a moment she considered telling him the lake was polluted, but his eagle eyes had spotted ripples in the water already, and then a stalking heron dipped its beak and raised its head triumphantly with a gleaming salmon.

'There are brown trout, salmon and sea trout in the demesne waters,' she said resignedly. He might as well know. If she had to sell, she'd darn well make sure she got a good price! 'The fishing is the best in the area. We get shoals of herring off the coast in October. And there are loads of bass off the Strand.'

'Ah. Bass. Good strong fighters.'

'I don't see you as a fisherman,' she said scornfully.

'No? Don't let my appearance fool you——' he began.

'It doesn't!' she snapped, unable to keep up the pretence.

'And what does that mean?' he asked in icy tones.

She faced him squarely, her legs a little apart and her hands planted angrily on her hips.

'All these questions! Picking up handfuls of soil! Wondering about the potential of the land! You're no writer,' she scorned. 'Just who are you?'

'If you hadn't sent your henchman to summon me so imperiously to your presence, I might have spared you this,' he said tightly. 'But you betrayed yourself for a haughty, cold and spoiled little rich girl. Ex-rich girl,' he amended with a sneer.

'Oh! You're pure evil! Only fools believe everything they read in the papers.'

'No smoke without fire.'

'You can get off my land! And I'm not giving you a lift back; you can darn well walk, injured leg or not!'

'Compassion isn't in your nature, is it?' he remarked, a hard light in his eyes.

'Not for snoopers like you. Ever since you arrived you've been intent on nosing around and, if you don't leave my demesne right away, I'll fetch Cormac to put you in your car!'

He laughed mockingly. 'I'll put him in hospital first,' he growled.

The threat was real. He actually believed he was stronger. Caitlin met his relentless gaze and her eyes widened. Something about him made her sure that he was, indeed, more than a match for Cormac, who only knew how to fight fair. This stranger would know every dirty trick in the book. The grim set of his face and the jutting jaw emphasised that, and she recognised in him the physical strength and confidence of a man who had been in action before. His body awareness wasn't just the result of an amateur keep-fit programme. Fitness was part of his profession, she was sure. What on earth could it be? And what was a man like him doing here?

'Who are you?' she whispered.

He gave a slight smile. 'You'll find out,' he promised, then turned briskly on his heel and strode in long, loping strides down the track, back to the long-house, his limp hardly noticeable, as if he were forcing himself to put his weight on his leg as a matter of pride.

Caitlin's temper was really aroused. She couldn't wait to get back and see what Cormac had discovered. When she did, she was so angry that she didn't want any lunch, and offered it to Cormac when she found him in the kitchen, sitting over a cup of coffee. He'd hardly taken a bite out of a ham roll when she began to interrogate him.

'Hang on, Cait!' he complained, his mouth full.

'Listen, you don't know how dangerous this man might be,' she raged. 'Tell me what you found!'

Cormac sighed and put down the roll. 'I don't know what's got into you. You've lost that nice calm manner. I know you're under pressure, but going off the rails won't help. Anyway, I found nothing. No sign of his identity at all. Only a huge deed-box which I couldn't open.'

'Oh, come on, there must have been something,' she said impatiently. 'A letter, a cheque-book, something!'

'Nothing,' he said, spreading his hands.

She sat back, thinking rapidly. 'You know, that's most peculiar,' she said. 'Everyone has things which identify them. It's almost as if he's hiding his identity on purpose.'

They both jumped as the back kitchen door slammed open, to reveal the stranger, furiously angry, striding in as if he owned the house and was about to throw them out bodily. They automatically shrank back at the force of his entry and his barely contained rage.

'How dare you?' he seethed. 'How dare you search my things?'

Caitlin and Cormac exchanged astonished glances.

'Oh, Cormac,' she said reproachfully. He'd promised not to disturb anything.

'What makes you think we've been in the long-house?' retaliated Cormac, giving her hand a reassuring squeeze.

So he hadn't left evidence. Caitlin gained her equilibrium again. 'And how dare you burst in here?' she declared coldly, rising to her feet. 'How did you get back so quickly, anyway?'

'Murphy gave me a lift,' he growled. 'Well, did you find anything?' he asked Cormac with a sneer.

'What evidence do you have that I looked?' he defied.

'I'm a cautious man. I know when people have touched my things. I take care to leave my belongings so I know if they're disturbed,' he snapped. 'And stop underestimating me. Hell! People's curiosity in these parts is excessive. When there's a whispered conversation between two people and one of them hurries off furtively and then I find my belongings have been moved, I am perfectly capable of putting the facts together and coming up with an answer.'

'All right,' said Caitlin defiantly. 'He did it on my orders.'

'Orders?'

She flushed. He was always making her sound like a dictatorial snob, and all she meant was that it wasn't Cormac's fault.

'You'd been acting very suspiciously. I wanted to know who you are and what you are doing here,' she said angrily.

'Send him away and I'll tell you,' he said in a furious tone.

'You think I'd leave her alone with you?' asked Cormac belligerently.

Caitlin put her hand on his arm. He looked as if he was going to strike the stranger, and she didn't want them fighting.

A bunch of keys was thrown on to the kitchen table. 'Go to the long-house. Look at the contents of my deed-box, make sure you understand their meaning and bring the box back here.'

Like everyone else, Cormac responded to the authoritative tone. Then he looked doubtfully at the keys he'd picked up. Caitlin gave a resigned sigh. At last the nagging doubts in her mind would be cleared up, one way or another. 'I'd like you to do that. I'll be all right. Please.'

Her legs were trembling and she steadied herself against the table, unnerved by the ominous expression on the stranger's face. Cormac slammed his way out.

There was a long silence which grew more loaded with tension every second as a pair of glittering eyes brooded at Caitlin from under lowered brows. She couldn't stand it any longer. Her pulses were racing unevenly and her throat was dry with nervous anticipation. He was going to tell her something awful, she knew from the harsh lines of his mouth and his taut body.

'Well?' she asked icily, with an arrogant arch to her brow.

The man regarded her cynically. 'What an insufferably superior woman you are! I hadn't wanted to tell you what I am doing here so soon. I intended to look around, bide my time and see what kind of person you were. But I think I've seen enough. Particularly enough of you.'

Enraged, she could bear his insinuations and browbeating no longer. She was sick to death of people misreading her character! With a sudden flurry of movement, she ran up to him and raised her hand to strike his smug face but, before she knew what was happening, he had whirled her around and twisted her arm behind her back, pulling her against his chest. For a moment the pain ran through her like a knife, and then he had loosened his hold and merely encircled her waist. But that was worse, since her spine lay lovingly against his hard-muscled body, as close as a second skin, and as she struggled she became aware of the flood of heat coming from his loins and the fact that her hair was slipping silkily across his face and he was breathing erotically into it.

'Let me go!' she jerked out, breathless from his crushing arm.

'When you've calmed down, and not before. Are you strong, Caitlin? I do hope so,' he murmured into her ear. His warm breath and the flurries of excitement it aroused made her flinch. 'You're going to need strength in the next few months. Unless you take the easy way out and marry Cormac.'

She was silent, hating his mockery. She was well aware of her unsettled future, and didn't need him to rub it in!

'No? He doesn't appeal? Too unsophisticated? How about living with a man educated in Geneva, with a flat in Paris, a villa in Mustique and who has spent half his life in Africa?'

Caitlin grew very still, knowing he was talking about himself. Why was he telling her all this? He turned her around slowly, but kept her a prisoner by grasping her arms, and she was too proud to ask him to release her.

Instead, she tilted her head up and fixed him with a scornful look.

His eyebrows lifted. 'Interested?'

'If you mean am I interested in you, the answer is no,' she said coldly.

'Really? You may change your mind later.' His fingers slid up her arms and one hand caught her chin, cupping it.

Her head reeled at the way he was looking at her, his eyes belying his cruel words, a fierce desire lurking in their depths. Despite herself, despite the fact that she hated this man and mistrusted him, her body responded to him. There was a raw potency in him that was exciting. To her dismay, she felt her breasts begin to rise and swell. Small tremors ran through to her toes, and strange spiralling waves trickled into every nerve.

His hand tightened. Then his mouth descended, and his fingers were spreading through her hair, cradling the back of her skull, as his lips ground harshly into hers in a terrifyingly, fiercely satisfying kiss that went on forever. She began to moan—wanting to escape or in a kind of release for the passion he was arousing? Whatever, whoever, he was, he had struck a chord within her that no other man had ever found, and she was incapable of preventing her hands from grabbing his head and forcing his mouth even harder on to hers. It was a primitive response, for all inhibitions were flung away in the wild, untamed way he kissed her, arousing in her an equally abandoned passion which knew no law, no bounds. With this man, she felt she could know an intensity of loving that her starved body demanded.

They staggered against the wall. His lips roamed freely over her face and throat, his fingers touring her shoulders, suddenly wrenching down her loose blouse and exposing the soft, smooth and rounded flesh where her breasts began to swell. With a groan, his lips savaged gently and then returned to her mouth, forcing it open with his moist tongue.

Then, before the tantalising prospect of invasion materialised, he seemed to check himself. Caitlin's hands fluttered helplessly at his chest, but he drew away, his breath rasping harshly.

His eyes blazed with hatred. Bewildered, Caitlin closed her eyes, trying to understand what had happened and why she had connived in her own assault. Every part of her body tingled, every inch reached out to him, even her poppy-bruised mouth.

'Hell!' He shook his head to clear it. 'The same trick that Piaras Ferriter fell for! How ironic! You scheming little madam! You *are* a "cheap woman of little virtue",' he scathed, repeating a quote made by a resentfully unsuccessful ex-boyfriend in the newspaper. 'Do you always respond like that? Or am I being specially honoured? Perhaps you were hoping to seduce me and gain some kind of advantage. I do believe, Caitlin, you know who I am after all.'

'I *don't*!' she wailed. 'I wish I did!' Anything was better than being confused, from wishing this hateful man would stop accusing her and kiss her again instead.

'Oh, come,' he scorned. 'Are you telling me you don't know I am here to take Cashelkerry from you?'

She stopped breathing as a jolt hurtled through her like a bolt of electricity. Oh, no! She'd been right! She winced from the physical pain burning in her chest.

'You . . . you intend to buy me out?' she whispered in horror.

'Buy?' He laughed mirthlessly, and Caitlin noticed that the hand he pushed into his pocket was shaking. 'I don't need to buy. I already own this land, and have done so for a while.'

She pressed her hands against the wall for support. The room whirled around her and she went white. Dimly she was aware that he had picked her up and carried her over to an easy chair and was rubbing her hands, a frown of angry concentration on his face.

She snatched her hands away and leaned towards him, searching for some sense in what he said, his words hammering over and over again in her head. It was impossible. He was playing with her again. What a swine he was!

'It's not true. It can't be true. You're lying.' She passed a muddled hand over her forehead.

'I really thought you knew,' he muttered.

'Stop it! I don't believe you! Father said nothing of this. The solicitor didn't tell me...'

'They said nothing because they believed I was dead. If I had been, then Cashel would have reverted to your father and therefore to you. But I turned up again, and so it is still mine.' He fixed her with his hard, merciless eyes and she cringed. He seemed very certain. 'Caitlin, this is not your house and it is not your land. It never was. You and your father, your grandfather and great-grandfather, were merely squatters.'

'How do you know this?' she whispered, appalled.

His smile was the smile of a winner.

'Because I am Jake Ferriter,' he said softly. 'I own Cashel.'

CHAPTER FOUR

A solid ball of nausea lay in Caitlin's cramping stomach. There was a roaring in her ears and she felt strangely heavy, as if she had turned to stone and would never rise from the chair again.

The strong smell of brandy came to her nose, and she looked down to see a glass being thrust at her. With a wild sweep of her hand she knocked the glass from Jake Ferriter's grip and dashed it to the ground where it shattered into tiny pieces. She stared at the pool of red-gold liquid on the flagstones and then slowly lifted her head.

'If you want to survive this day, Mr Ferriter,' she whispered, 'I suggest that you get out of here and into that flashy red car of yours, and don't stop driving until you've left Ireland far behind you.'

'Such an intensity of feeling! So you are a woman of emotion,' he mocked. 'Passionate in the desire to maintain your social position.'

Caitlin's eyes blazed with hatred. 'I won't let you crush me! I refuse to believe a word you've said. But if you are really Jake Ferriter, then you're responsible for my father's death, and for that I'll never forgive you!'

Jake frowned. 'You can't believe that, Caitlin. You know what caused your father's death, and I had nothing to do with it. Even if I hadn't been around, it would have happened.'

'That's not true!' she accused heatedly. 'You, with your life-draining, slow-dripping poison, making Father think we had no right to the land...'

'You didn't!' he snapped. 'None at all! Everything that happened to your family has been of its own making. I refuse to accept responsibility for the O'Connells!'

Caitlin launched herself at him and he jumped back, but her attack was so hysterical that for a moment she was beating at his chest, hammering her fists into his unyielding body, and then he had pinioned her arms again and her eyes were inches from his stern mouth.

Gradually her anger receded, to be replaced by sheer exhaustion. She slumped in his arms and he picked her up effortlessly, striding determinedly out into the hall and moving towards the stairs.

'Where are you taking me?' she whispered, frightened, a prisoner in his grip. The pulses in her body had begun to leap into life again.

'To bed,' he growled.

She gasped. 'No! I don't want——'

He interrupted her with a short, mirthless laugh. 'Your desires are very obvious.'

Caitlin felt her body weaken from the warmth of his chest and strength in his arms. His face was very close, the tanned, angled jaw an unnerving temptation. He had aroused her dormant sexuality and left it unsatisfied and now, with every movement of his virile, masculine body, she was reminded of his potential passion. And hers. Within her raged a fire whose existence she had never suspected. No longer could she think of herself as essentially a cool, even-blooded woman.

Jake Ferriter had proved to be a master of seduction. Only he had succeeded in touching the white heat of her passion. Only he had discovered it was there. Of all men to know! It made her terribly vulnerable to him; it gave him the advantage. His worldly, sexual experience meant that he could humiliate her by using her own unwilling, treacherous response to him as a weapon.

'You dare try anything!' she choked, as he kicked open the door at the top of the stairs, rightly judging it must be the master bedroom.

He dumped her unceremoniously on the scarlet counterpane and eyed her mockingly. 'I'm not the kind of man to try,' he murmured. 'I succeed.'

'I'll yell if you come one step nearer,' she threatened.

'As you like. But I happen to know that your house-keeper has gone shopping and it'll be a little while before Cormac returns to show you what he's found in my deed-box. In the meantime,' he moved menacingly closer and she shrank back into the pillows, '—yes, Caitlin, you are right to be afraid of me. I wield power over you. More, I think, than you imagine. Beginning to believe me now?' he snapped.

'What—what are you going to do?' she breathed.

His callous eyes seemed to strip her until the heat ran like fire in her veins.

'Hell, you would tempt a monk,' he said huskily. He sat down on the bed and, when she flung her head away so that she didn't have to look into his wicked green eyes, he slid the palm of his hand down her cheek and forced her to meet his gaze. 'I will endeavour to keep my hands off you and tell you how and why I own Cashel. That is...' His hand trailed down her throat, stroking along the collar-bone. Caitlin felt unable to breathe. 'That is, if you want to hear.'

'Yes, yes, I do!' she croaked. Anything to keep his mind off seducing her! She knew she couldn't hold out against him for long, if he really put his mind to possessing her. She just seemed to melt when he touched her body. To her utter relief, he sat back and folded his arms, an inscrutable expression on his face.

'I didn't know of my Irish descent until my father died of cancer two years ago. My mother had long divorced him and vanished from our lives. Adultery,' he said, at Caitlin's querying look. 'I found family papers. They interested me, particularly when I discovered that the land had been unjustly seized by the O'Connells.' His eyes narrowed at her baleful look. 'It was even more interesting to discover that your father was deeply in debt. He'd invested unwisely and your education and expenses were proving to be a burden.'

'I had no idea,' she whispered miserably.

'Maybe. Anyway, I had my agent suggest to him that he could clear his debts and free the estate of future death duties by selling Cashel, providing, of course, that he lived for the requisite number of years after the sale. There was much secrecy. He wanted to keep his position. There were only a few selected buyers and we bid by envelope. Do you know what that means?'

Caitlin shook her head dumbly, a growing fear within her. Father hadn't told her the whole truth. Jake was doing just that, though, in those business-like, emotionless words. Her whole world was crashing about her ears.

'Those selected to bid put their offers in sealed envelopes. That way no one but the agents knew who bid and how much was offered. I made sure that my bid was generous. My agent thought Cashel had a value over and above sentiment.'

'Sentiment?' blurted Caitlin.

'Oh, yes,' he murmured, his bold eyes holding her mesmerised. 'Owning my ancestral land, which my family had been forced to abandon, was important to me.'

'No one made them go! They left in the Famine, of their own accord!' she retorted.

'I hope that's what you sincerely believe and not one of your practised lies,' snapped Jake. 'The historical evidence is that your ancestors carried out a systematic and determined witch-hunt till the Ferriters were driven out. It's a sweet moment, Caitlin, to return!'

'You don't need to see me as the object of your revenge. I've done nothing to you,' she muttered. 'Father said the money went on a legal battle, when he tried to claim Cashel by the law of squatters' rights.'

'He only talked of that,' replied Jake. 'I told him that if he won such an action, he would still be in debt and wouldn't be able to hang on to Cashel. I offered him a way out. He saved his pride and continued to live on the land for a while.'

'I don't understand. If Father sold to you, why didn't you take over straight away? And where's the money? And why didn't our solicitor tell me about all this?' She flashed him a triumphant look. Get out of that, Jake Ferriter! He wasn't dealing with a fool, whatever he thought of women!

'For the moment I was content merely to own Cashel,' he said laconically. 'My business interests were far too involved to consider coming to Ireland. Besides, the deal was that your father could live here, paying a peppercorn rent, until his death, and then I or my descendants would take over. His death occurred sooner than any of us expected. As for the money—well, he invested badly again. He wasn't a businessman, Caitlin,' he said more gently.

'There must be some money left,' she said tremulously.

'Very little, I'm afraid. What he imagined to be your dowry has dwindled to a paltry sum. His losses depressed him, I think. He certainly was unable to keep his part of the bargain with me.'

'What bargain?' she cried bitterly. 'A bargain with the devil?'

'He lived here on the understanding that he efficiently maintained Cashel House and the demesne. This he failed to do and I tried to get possession, but there was a lengthy legal battle again. Then I disappeared. Everyone thought I was dead and therefore our contract was null and void. He thought he was safe.'

'I wish to hell you'd never come back!' breathed Caitlin.

'Thank you for those charming words,' grated Jake. 'When I did return to civilisation, I had an urge to give up certain aspects of my work and live in a different way. I was about to buy an estate in Scotland when I heard that—despite the presence of an excellent manager, Cormac Kelly—the value of Cashel had decreased dramatically and your father was running it into the ground. Perhaps it amused him to do so. I don't know.'

'He'd never have wanted you here, I'm certain of that!' she flashed.

'As I thought. Anyway, I told him he'd reneged on his duty and I was intending to move in whether he liked it or not.'

Caitlin's heart thudded painfully. 'And then he died,' she whispered, appalled, her huge eyes glistening.

'Yes. For that I'm sorry. He didn't give me a chance to explain what I was going to do about you both.'

'It was your telephone call,' she said, barely audible. 'You told him that terrible news and he died. You *were* responsible for his death! Murderer!' she yelled hysterically. 'Murderer!'

Heavy footsteps pounded up the stairs and Cormac burst in. He looked at the couple, frozen in hatred—Caitlin's eyes wild, Jake's dark and exasperated.

'Caitlin! What on earth are you yelling about? Have you lost your senses?' demanded Cormac.

She turned rebellious eyes to him. He didn't like the real woman beneath the calm! She could tell he found her over-excited state embarrassing.

'It's an understandable reaction after all she's been through lately. Show her the documents you've been reading,' said Jake. 'Help her to read them and explain them to her. Then I want you to gather all the staff in the library. I'll be there in an hour to make my announcement and tell them what the new situation will be.'

'And me? Where will I go?' cried Caitlin. 'What will happen to me?'

Jake sighed. 'You'll stay here, of course, and try to get Cashel back. I wouldn't expect anything less of you. It could be rather enjoyable.'

'You bastard!' swore Cormac.

'Careful. You have a position to lose. Or do you want to give in your notice now?'

'You know that jobs like this are impossible to find,' seethed Caitlin. 'He has no choice.'

Jake's cynical eyes bored into the hapless Cormac. 'You're an efficient and trustworthy manager, if a little too reluctant to tell your former boss that his orders were unsuitable. I'd like to keep your services and send you on a course in land management. I think your wages are too low and am offering you double. Take it or leave it, but let me know when you come downstairs.' He nodded towards Caitlin. 'Keep an eye on her. She's had quite a shock.'

Caitlin's mind was whirling at his clipped, business-like manner. She watched him leave, thinking that he seemed to know exactly what he was doing and what he wanted, which was a lot more than she did! She turned bemused eyes to Cormac.

He was frowning. 'What shall I do, Cait? Do you want me to work for him, or not? Shall I go?'

The idea of being in the house alone with Jake Ferriter, filled her with panic.

'No, don't leave!' she begged. 'I need a friend! I don't know if I'll stay myself, but until I can think straight, I want you near. Please, Cormac, don't go!'

'Oh, Cait!' he muttered, settling on the bed and taking her in his arms. 'I'll look after you, you know that.'

'How sweet,' came Jake's sardonic tones from the door.

Caitlin pushed Cormac away in fury. 'Is it a habit of yours to be always sneaking around and interrupting private conversations?' she raged.

'I forgot something,' he said mildly. 'I meant to tell you that I regard this as my bedroom now. It is, after all, the master bedroom. You can stay, of course, if you like, providing you don't snore.'

Her mouth dropped open in amazement. 'Of course I don't snore!' she spluttered. Before she could continue, he broke in.

'Is that true, Cormac?' he asked innocently.

'How the hell would I know?' Cormac glared.

Jake smiled in a satisfied way. 'I prefer the right side of the bed,' he said, starting to leave again.

'Have the right, left and centre,' grated Caitlin. 'I'll move out of here immediately.'

'Pity,' said Jake. 'It looks like being a cold night.'

'Now, look here——' began Cormac.

'Hurry up and go through those documents,' ordered Jake. 'And get the staff mustered. I'm a busy man.'

Caitlin had moved into her old room and she should have felt comfortable there, but she didn't. She'd quickly become used to sleeping in a double bed and having plenty of space to sprawl.

In the morning she woke early, at dawn, shaky after a fitful sleep filled with nightmares. When it was obvious that she was wide awake and unlikely to get any more rest, she stumbled from the bed and blearily drew the curtains.

Outside on the lawn, Jake Ferriter was exercising. Caitlin watched sullenly. He wore a pair of track-suit bottoms and trainers, the pale rosy glow of the dawn lighting his torso and making the bunching muscles gleam. The sheen on his skin indicated that he'd been working out for some time. His body moved easily and lithely, and she was reluctantly forced into admiration at the way he drove himself in the punishing routine.

Then, as he rose from a completed set of press-ups, he saw her at the window. She withdrew hastily, conscious of the flimsiness of her silk nightie, with its tiny straps and deep-cut bodice. But already his eyes had grown hot and she retained the image of him, powerful, threateningly sexy and intensely masculine.

Angrily she went to the small bathroom and stripped, scrubbing herself viciously as she tried to subdue her flaring nerves. She really couldn't live in the same house! She hated him—hated his ruthlessness, his deceit, his revenge, and above all the way he had ruined her father.

Caitlin took a long time deciding what to wear. Eventually she decided on a baggy shirt and a pair of old jeans. Although she wanted make-up as a mask and a defence, she decided to keep herself as plain and un-attractive as possible. She scraped her hair back to the top of her head, fastened it with combs and hurried down, hoping she might eat breakfast alone.

Her throat constricted at the sight of Jake, fresh and glowing from his shower, already helping himself to scrambled eggs from the silver server on the dining-room sideboard. He wore a pair of well-cut black trousers, the jacket resting on the chair at the head of the table. His white shirt lay open at the neck, his tie carelessly half-hitched. He looked devastatingly handsome and Caitlin had to force herself to appear unaffected.

'Morning, Caitlin,' he said softly. 'You look a little sleepy-eyed. Does that mean you've been up all night, thinking?'

She glared, and he laughed. 'Help yourself,' he said generously, waving his hand at the selection of dishes.

Caitlin almost choked with fury and misery. He certainly believed in making his ownership clear. And what had he done with Cormac? They'd got into the habit of eating breakfast together, discussing what they would work on that day.

'I don't usually breakfast alone,' she began.

'I bet you don't,' he said tightly.

She bristled at his tone. 'I mean that Cormac is usually here.'

'He's already working, on my instructions,' said Jake, seating himself at the head of the table.

Caitlin pointedly moved the cutlery so that she was as far away from him as possible, and began to eat in silence.

'You'll have to talk to me sometime,' Jake observed.

She flashed him an icy look and took a deep interest in her food.

'We have many things to discuss. For instance, are any of your friends likely to appear?'

'What?' she asked, in surprise. Why should he worry about that?

'Are they?' he insisted.

She thought with a pang that none of her so-called friends had been near her since the news of her father's death had been published.

'I think they're respecting my grief,' she said pointedly, reminding him that he ought to treat her gently.

'Of course. That's probably the reason,' he said suavely, plainly not thinking that at all. 'It's just that I don't want anyone to know that I'm here—or, at least, that Jake Ferriter is here.'

'Why? Are you wanted by the police? Or irate husbands?' she scathed.

A smile touched his lips and then vanished. 'Only our respective legal advisers and your father knew that I'd disappeared. I own a group of leisure centres and associated companies, and shares would have tumbled if anyone had known. In a while the story can come out, but I don't want media interest now—and I'm sure you don't, either, Caitlin.'

'No, I don't,' she said fervently, remembering how awful it had been to be pestered. 'But you might tell me what happened to you—why people thought you were dead.'

'I was unavoidably detained in Angola,' he said laconically, eyeing her over his coffee-cup.

'For a year?' She frowned, remembering what he had said earlier.

'Yes.'

Caitlin studied his closed face and then the penny dropped. 'Prison!' she stated triumphantly.

'Correct.' His expression grew even more remote and rather frightening as she wondered nervously what he had done to warrant a prison sentence of that duration. 'I can be a dangerous man, Caitlin,' he said in an undertone, confirming her thoughts. 'Don't cross me. It's unwise. Very unwise.'

Suddenly she saw that her hand was shaking and she put down her knife and fork with a clatter, pushing away her plate and her half-eaten breakfast. As far as battles of will went, he was winning hands down! The news of his prison sentence had shocked her. There were sinister depths to Jake Ferriter, and she disliked the idea of a man like him owning Cashelkerry. He wasn't the sort to be a gentleman farmer. Some unpleasant, unsuitable scheme was obviously in the making. Caitlin shivered.

There was a knock on the door, a rather hesitant one.

'Come in!' called Jake, still watching her intently.

'I've put the files you wanted on the desk in the study,' said Cormac, his hands big and awkward at his sides. Caitlin had the impression he was trying not to see her.

'Thank you,' said Jake. Then he turned his head and scanned Cormac's hang-dog face. 'Aren't you going to greet your mistress? Or have you already seen her this morning?' he asked silkily.

Cormac went bright red. 'Morning, Caitlin,' he mumbled.

She was incensed, and decided to turn the tables. 'Morning, Cormac. Come and sit beside me and let's chatter about what we're going to do together as we usually do.'

He looked a little puzzled, and very confused, as if he wasn't sure whether to join her or not.

'Cormac has had breakfast,' said Jake in a disapproving way. 'And he has work to do for me. Start stock-taking now. Is everyone ready?'

'Yes, they're all pretty eager,' said Cormac enthusiastically. 'They've talked of nothing but your plans, ever since . . .'

'Good. Fine. Thank you. I'll be with you later. There are one or two things I want to discuss with Caitlin.'

He waited until Cormac had gone before rising purposefully. Caitlin poured herself another cup of tea and wished she hadn't, because she was sure he'd notice how her hand trembled. So, she thought sadly, his plans were exciting! They must be something special to have made Cormac go over to the enemy like that. And what were Jake Ferriter's plans for her?

'My ex-employees seem to have been impressed by you,' she said coldly.

'Maybe they know something you don't,' he said quietly.

'So tell me,' she said, unnerved by the fact that he was pacing up and down behind her chair, his stride strong and steady as if he had never been injured.

A pair of hands gripped the back of the chair by her head, and she tensed at the nearness of his body.

'What do you think of Cormac?' he asked softly.

She tried not to react to the way his breath had fluttered over the top of her head, making the hairs on her scalp rise.

'In what way?' she asked cautiously.

'I want to know if you're likely to marry him.'

'That's none of your business!'

'It could be.' He came to her side and then leaned back against the table with folded arms, his thighs tantalisingly close. 'If you are considering the idea, or are thinking of giving up Cashel and dashing off to some jet-setting boyfriend in Marbella, I won't make my offer.'

Her head lifted slowly. As it did so, she hungered for his virile body. Hating herself, her eyes ran in slow yearning over the narrow hips, his deep chest and the sweet hollow in his throat set off by the immaculate white shirt.

'What offer?' she asked huskily.

He held out his hand. 'Come and see, Caitlin,' he said, a serious note in his voice.

Their eyes met and held. Beneath his hooded lids was a drowsy look which had liquefied his eyes into green chartreuse. Tiny threads of nerves awoke in her body. They turned into ropes, twisting in warm, curling coils. Then suddenly it seemed her hand had met his and was captured, she was gently pulled to her feet and she was thinking wildly that his grip was like hot, pulsating steel.

If she moved one hair's breadth, she would be plastered against his body.

A masculine desire filled his face, his lashes fluttering lazily as he watched her bemused reaction.

'You are very beautiful, Caitlin,' he murmured. 'Very beautiful, and very desirable.'

'In these clothes? You're mocking me! I purposely didn't dress up. I mean I...'

He laughed softly and she was treated to his dazzling smile which gentled his face and caused her weakness to grow.

'No clothes can hide your loveliness. But I'm fascinated that you should try.'

'I...' She swallowed away the lump in her throat, wishing the unbearable ache in her body would go too. 'Please let go of my hand.'

To her contrary disappointment, he did so. 'Well, Caitlin? Are you in love with any man? Are you intending to leave Cashel? You can stay here, under certain conditions, you know.'

Love? she thought dazedly, transfixed by the sexy curve of his mouth. She tried to concentrate instead on what he had said. 'You know I don't want to leave Cashel,' she said in an undertone, moistening her dry lips and trying not to notice the way his sensual eyes brooded on that movement. 'But I can't stay here with you in the house. Why don't you go off to your other businesses and leave me here in my father's place? I can manage the land. Cormac said I was picking up methods very well.'

He'd frowned at Cormac's name. 'I've grown tired of sitting at desks in different parts of the world,' he said quietly. 'Last year, when I was in Angola, I thought a great deal and realised that the only time I was really happy was when I worked on the land and mixed high-powered business with physical exertion.'

'You worked on the land?' she exclaimed, her eyes widening.

'Sort of,' he said, mocking the answer she once gave him with an exaggerated Irish accent. She glared at him resentfully and he smiled. 'Irritating, isn't it? Especially when you're dying to have some information. Come on, I'll put you out of your misery. I'll show you what I have to offer.'

Caitlin threw him a suspicious look, alerted by the amusement in his voice. He really was a devil, the way he played with her!

She followed him crossly into the study. A stack of files lay on her father's desk and she steeled herself to seeing him take his place there. But then she saw that the small desk from the library had been placed in the window and it was there that he led her.

'This,' he said, picking up a rough sketch, 'is my plan for Cashelkerry. The staff have given their unanimous approval and now I want yours.'

'You showed them before me?' she asked bitterly.

'I didn't want to upset you with it if it was tasteless or unsuitable,' he replied gently. 'But they thought you'd like it.'

'Why should my approval be of any interest to you?' she asked.

'Because I want you to be part of it,' he answered. 'It wouldn't be the same without you.'

Caitlin didn't know what to say. His concern, and his professed desire to want her to take a special part in his plans, could be quite false. Yet there was a wealth of sincerity in his tone that made her tremble. She took the sketch from his hand and stared at it blindly.

'Here.' His hand pressed into the small of her back and he had pushed her to the window, standing far too close. 'The house will be restored, but left much as it is. I'll need more parking, and that will be here.' His long finger traced an area to one side of Cashel House. 'This will be the helicopter landing pad . . .'

Caitlin tried to take in what he was saying. There were to be equipment sheds in the old barns, canoe houses on the lake, the jetty was to be lengthened . . .

'What is all this for?' she asked shakily.

Jake laughed in apology. 'I'm sorry. I'm so excited by the idea. Cashel is perfect and I can't wait to get started. No—I'm not prevaricating!' He grinned, his eyes shining with delight. 'I just feel a bit light-headed.'

So did she. But it was his proximity causing that! Caitlin's nerves were strung taut.

'Explain to me,' she muttered.

'It'll be wonderful,' he said eagerly, taking hold of her shoulders in his excitement. 'I intend to turn Cashel into an executives' Survival School. I ran one in Tunisia and it's still going. They're turning business away. Companies send their top management on toughening-up courses; it improves their managerial performance dramatically.'

'You mean you'll have dozens of people coming here and playing Boy Scouts?' she frowned.

'And Girl Guides.' He smiled, not noticing her doubts. 'They'll learn to live off the land, coping with the various problems I throw their way. They'll find out how to work in a team and how leaders are thrown up. We can get them to build temporary bridges over the river, abseil down the cliff—and none of this will alter the ap-

pearance of Cashel much, yet there'll be plenty of employment on offer. I gather unemployment is a problem
around here.'

'Yes,' she said slowly. Now she knew why the staff
had been so excited and why Cormac had thrown his lot
in with Jake Ferriter. Even she felt something of Jake's
eagerness.

'Where do I come in?' she asked. 'Dishing out hard
hats and seasickness pills?'

The grip on her shoulders tightened imperceptibly as
he chuckled. Caitlin was totally disarmed by the exuberance in his face.

'Not quite! The way I've run this set-up in the past is
to give a welcoming party and a briefing when the
executives arrive. There's one hell of a shindig at the
end, too. Everyone's inhibitions have melted after
spending a few nights out in the rain, huddling behind
a wall for shelter.'

Caitlin recognised in a flash everything he'd been
searching for, when she'd showed him around the estate.
Yet she still didn't see where she fitted.

'Caitlin,' he urged, stepping even closer, 'I want you
to act as my hostess. I need someone to organise the
parties, the food, the whole presentation of the house.'

'You could do that,' she said nervously, frightened of
being part of this venture. It made him too elated, too
appealing.

'No. I'll be far too busy taking part,' he said.

'You? Abseiling down that cliff?' Horror edged her
tone and she faltered at the tender light in his eyes.

'Don't worry about me. I'm far tougher than this
formal attire would suggest. I love adventure—crave it.

I get high on adrenalin. I need spice.' His voice grew husky. 'Especially spice,' he said wickedly.

'Did you have a hostess in Tunisia?' she asked, feeling a stab of anger at the thought. Jealousy! Now, what on earth had caused that? She couldn't possibly envy some other woman sharing his thrills. Or causing them, she thought with mounting agitation.

'Oh, a harem of them,' he grinned. 'Sadly, it's impossible to import harems. You can't get an import licence for them.'

Caitlin wasn't sure whether he was joking or not. She wouldn't put anything past Jake Ferriter!

'I can't appear in this house as your hostess,' she said with regret. It sounded fun, and she'd dearly love to be involved in the redecoration of Cashel—and to witness the way he ran the Survival School.

'I want you to, very much,' he said softly.

'No. It's out of the question.'

'What will you do, then? What are your qualifications?'

She dropped her lashes. 'None. With Mother and Patrick dying just before my exams, I was unable to study. I failed every exam in the end.'

'So you're good for nothing but gracing my table.' He smiled mockingly. 'You have no money and no prospect of a job—letting the long-house won't keep you in underwear. We've already established that there isn't a potential husband on the horizon to take care of you. You'd better make do with me.'

'What do you mean?' she asked quickly. By his languorous tone, he wasn't talking about working for him now.

'As I said, I would like you to be my hostess. You are incredibly beautiful, have a natural grace and your social flitting around has given you the ability to handle yourself. You won't be tongue-tied or awkward with high-level executives. But there's something else, Caitlin. Something quite unconnected.'

Her eyes drifted over his sensually curving mouth. She swayed a little from the potency of his body. A whirlwind of emotions was storming through her head and she struggled to keep herself from lifting her lips to demand his hard, satisfying kiss.

'What?' she croaked.

'You know,' he whispered, his index finger touching her full mouth. Despite herself, her lips parted and became pouting. 'You know very well that I want you. I'm resisting the urge to kiss you because you need to answer with your head and not be persuaded by my lips. But I want you to stay here as the mistress of Cashel. My mistress, Caitlin. Then,' he breathed, 'I will have everything I want. You will have Cashel, too. You'll preside over a beautiful house, and I will protect you. I will also make love to you like no man has before, I can promise you that. There is an excitement between us I've never felt before. A sexual chemistry and a tension which cries out for action.' His eyes glittered febrilely. 'That makes my adrenalin run and my veins pound more than anything I've ever known. Be my mistress, Caitlin. Let me be your lover!'

CHAPTER FIVE

JAKE'S suggestion had hit Caitlin like a bombshell. Yes, she had recognised the flame that had been kindled between them, even admitted to herself that he was the kind of man she might fall for. But the idea of being his kept woman was unthinkable!

She had frozen into a statue, only the gradual stiffening of her body indicating any sign of response.

'Do you honestly think I would exchange my body for a roof over my head?' she grated.

'It's not any roof. It's Cashel. And I thought it would give you an excuse.'

'A what?' she cried, aghast. 'I don't need any excuse!'

'Not even to yourself?' he murmured.

'*No.* I couldn't let you touch me! You've gone too far, Jake Ferriter, in treating me like one of your cheap whores!'

His eyes blistered her with their intensity, all his softness, his sensuality, turned to a controlled fury.

'Oh, come, Caitlin. I thought you held your body cheaply. What's the difference between me in your bed and some lad you met skiing, ten minutes earlier?' He swept a calculating glance over her which increased Caitlin's anger. 'Apart from skill and pleasure, of course.'

'Even if I did hold my body cheaply,' she seethed, 'it wouldn't be so valueless as to submit to you.'

He shrugged. 'Pity. I really believed... well, it was worth a try,' he said casually.

'You're disgusting! Get some other woman to fill your bed!'

'I will. I merely thought you'd rather not have a succession of women acting as mistress here,' he said in a tone of challenge, as if deliberately trying to provoke her.

Her chest rose with an exasperated intake of breath. Of course she didn't want that! Bitterly she realised that she didn't want any woman in his bed at all, and now she'd given him *carte blanche* to introduce a stream of willing females! With a dignified tilt to her head, she forced herself to remain calm.

'If you behave like a rake, no one around here will work for you,' she said quietly.

'My earlier offer still stands,' said Jake. 'I can sublimate my passions if necessary. But I still want a hostess.'

'You have a nerve, after what you've just suggested!' she snapped.

'Forget it. A miscalculation. I would have thought plenty of men had propositioned you. Most sophisticated women would laugh it off. Or is it that the offer was tempting? Or threatening to you in any way?'

Caitlin turned her back on him and thought rapidly. He didn't know what she felt or he wouldn't have given up so easily. He'd been looking for a willing woman to satisfy him, and thought she was sexually experienced and therefore a good bet. Now she'd refused, he would try elsewhere. Men of the world, with dozens of potential partners, didn't trouble to pursue unwilling ones. If she made a big thing of this, he'd wonder why she was so offended—as he said, being propositioned was normal.

Normal in his world, she thought glumly. Power was supposed to be a great aphrodisiac—and Jake Ferriter had power, that was for sure. He had the looks, and sex appeal. Almost any other woman would take pity on him; he must be missing the heady, permissive life dreadfully. No, she couldn't turn down the job because he'd invited her to share his bed. It would seem as if she feared him. And she was darned if she wanted him to think that he had disturbed her emotions!

In addition, she reasoned, the alternative open to her wasn't too pleasant. If she didn't work for him, she'd have to leave Cashel, and she had nowhere to go. Pride prevented her from asking any of her wealthy, fair-weather friends to take pity on her, and she felt now that she couldn't go back to nothing but parties and bright chatter, anyway. Cashel had captured her totally. And its master.

With a quick movement to her mouth, to stifle a gasp, she realised that Jake Ferriter had woven a spell around her, trapping her into being an unwilling, helpless admirer. She admired him physically, mentally, and hungered for him emotionally. Only the spiritual dimension was lacking, and that had fortunately saved her from lying at his feet and melting into his arms, as countless other women had probably done, when he'd asked them to share his life for a brief time.

She had to stay. She couldn't tear herself away. And the coldness she felt for him now would protect her.

'If I take on this job,' she said, in a remote tone, 'I do it on certain conditions.'

'Name them.' Nothing betrayed what he felt about her potential decision.

'You make no more improper suggestions to me and you treat me like a lady.'

'Agreed.'

'I have complete control over the domestic running of the house and total freedom in planning the parties. I want no casual slut of yours to tell me what to do in Cashel.'

'Agreed.'

Now she knew he was grinning, but steeled herself to ignore that. He was an outrageous man!

'My private life is my own affair. Who I choose to bring to the house and what I choose to do in my spare time is no business of yours.'

'Of course,' he said smoothly. 'In fact, providing you keep the house up to a certain standard of efficiency and create an elegant atmosphere of welcome and two parties a fortnight, any other time is your own. Do what you please—although I'll have to work closely with you, of course, so that you can talk knowledgeably and charmingly to our paying guests.'

She flung him a frowning glance over her shoulder, but he looked innocent enough. That was a reasonable request, she supposed.

'And you need to know what we'll be doing and where we'll be each day, so there'll be a conference meeting over breakfast,' he said evenly. 'I always did that with my hostesses.'

Caitlin grated her teeth silently. 'And Cormac?'

'You leave him to me. He is my manager and you need have nothing to do with him,' he said in a warning tone.

She wondered what Cormac would think of having such a ruthless and demanding boss. 'My salary?' she asked.

'Let's begin with a retainer, shall we? Then you can decide whether you want to continue after a period of, say, two months after we've been in operation. Until then, I'll need your advice on décor and the development, though if past projects are anything to go by and I pull technicians from my own companies, we'll be under way very quickly. I don't believe in hanging around once I've set my sights on something. I get the groundwork done and then swing into full operation. That ensures success.' He gave her a brilliant grin. 'I'm expecting some of my own executives this afternoon. Treat us to tea and charm. I'll give you a preliminary contract after that.'

'If I behave nicely?' she asked sarcastically.

'Something like that,' he smiled. 'I think you'll enjoy it all, Caitlin. You're born to be a mistress.'

'Will you stop using that word?' she snapped.

Jake laughed wickedly. 'Sorry. It amuses me in a very childish way. I too must learn to behave myself. It's not too easy. I'm used to being rather unconventional. Well, excuse me, I must see how the stock-taking is progressing. I need figures for my valuer and the insurance manager this afternoon.'

'How many will be coming?' asked Caitlin, thinking she'd better organise some cake. Her mind raced ahead, and suddenly her eyes glinted. She'd provide a proper tea for him, if that was what he wanted. The pride of the O'Connells rose within her. She'd show him how well she could cope!

'The valuer, insurance manager, stud manager, lakes consultant and my accountant. And a secretary.'

She raised her brows. 'You didn't waste much time last night, did you?'

Jake chuckled. 'Well, I wasn't doing anything else. Like you, I found it hard to sleep. The excitement, you know.'

With that barb, he turned on his heel and strode out, his shoulders shaking suspiciously. Caitlin vowed that one of these days she would win one of their encounters!

She and Brigit enjoyed preparing for the visitors enormously. They made the hall welcoming with huge displays of wild flowers and grasses, and Caitlin asked for a peat fire to be lit later in the drawing-room. She had baked some scones and a chocolate cake, while Brigit rolled out the pastry for jam tarts and kept an eye on her malt bread in the oven. Mid-afternoon, Caitlin arranged everything ready on the tea-trolley and went up to change, leaving Brigit to make savoury sandwiches.

From her window, Caitlin could see the helicopter land and disgorge its occupants. The men looked immaculate in dark business suits and, when she saw the smart blonde secretary, she was glad that she'd put on an elegantly cut dress the colour of soft, green grass.

She checked her smooth, shining knot of hair and hurried downstairs to greet the visitors, delighted with their evident admiration. They were all generous in their praise of the tea, and tucked in with gusto, even the sophisticated-looking secretary.

'We have two kinds of tea,' said Caitlin. 'Lemon tea or Irish.'

'Irish?' queried Jake. 'I didn't know there were tea bushes in the Emerald Isles.'

'There aren't,' smiled Caitlin. 'It's the way we make it. Strong enough to trot a mouse on.'

They all laughed and she was kept busy dispensing tea while Jake outlined what he wanted them to do over the next few days. She went cold. He hadn't said they were staying! Earlier, when the helicopter had landed, she had turned away from the window to put the finishing touches to her appearance, and had obviously missed seeing their luggage being unloaded. How thoughtless of him! She'd need to get word to Brigit, and yet she couldn't leave their guests. Her mind ranged over the problems of airing bedrooms which hadn't been used for a while.

Something else occurred to her. Jake didn't have a secretary. He must need one, with all the work he was planning. Although she knew he did an enormous amount of business by phone—every time it was used, the kitchen extension lit up—he must surely find it necessary to confirm or elaborate in writing. The attractive blonde could become a permanent feature!

All the time, she'd been half listening to the stud manager, who was telling her about his job in Florida and how he was looking forward to buying ponies for Cashelkerry. She nodded absently at his plans to restore the stables and yard, and then suddenly she was aware that his tone had changed. It had become quieter, huskier.

'What did you say?' she asked with a pleasant smile, realising he was waiting for an answer. 'I'm sorry, I missed that last remark—I remembered something I had to do.'

'I asked if you'd decided where we are all sleeping,' he murmured, his eyes on her red lips.

'You're in the long-house,' broke in Jake. 'You and Ted. We're not yet organised as far as the bedrooms are concerned.'

With an inner smile, Caitlin realised that the two he'd billeted in the long-house were the only men under the age of forty! He must think she was a danger to the morals of his staff!

'Perhaps you'd like to let everyone else know where they're sleeping.' She smiled sweetly, wondering what he'd do about the blonde, who'd been crossing and re-crossing her long, silken legs and had attracted a great deal of attention. Perhaps, she thought, with uncharac-teristic sharpness, the woman would be treated to a per-sonal tour of the master bedroom.

'I've told Brigit,' said Jake. 'She'll take them all to their rooms after tea.'

So, thought Caitlin rebelliously under her smooth ex-terior, he'd gone over her head! She'd remind him pri-vately who was boss in the house!

'That was sweet of you to let her know,' she purred, cutting Ted a third slice of cake. 'It saved me the trouble.'

'It occurred to me you might not have realised that everyone was staying. You were in the bath when I came to tell you,' explained Jake. 'I didn't walk in. I know how you hate to be disturbed.'

There was a momentary silence. Caitlin knew he had deliberately pretended to claim some kind of intimate knowledge of her, in order that the men wouldn't trespass on what they imagined to be his territory. Her irritation was tempered by a secret satisfaction at seeing the sec-retary look sulky.

The stud manager had sat further back in his chair and fixed a polite smile on his face in place of the rakish expression. Jake was very clever, thought Caitlin. They wouldn't dare flirt with their boss's woman! He really was quite utterly without conscience.

The conversation swung back to Jake's plans and Caitlin became caught up in everyone's excitement. She forgot the petty annoyance and even forgot to be coolly gracious. Jake's men seemed to be almost as high-powered and quick-thinking as he was, and that made for a lively tea party. The secretary sank into the background as Caitlin answered questions about the area with enthusiasm, a glowing warmth in her eyes.

Then they all dispersed to their respective rooms to unpack and consider their objectives for the next few days. Caitlin began to stack the plates on the trolley and Jake came over to help.

'It was a marvellous spread, and you were a perfect hostess,' he smiled. 'Thank you.'

Inside she felt delighted with his approval. 'It's my job,' she said calmly.

'I can still thank you for doing it well. By the way, watch where my stud manager leads you. He is married, and he tends to roam. I think his job makes him restless!'

'Don't tell me who to associate with,' she said coldly.

'You may be used to ruining marriages, but he's a good worker and I don't want any trouble,' frowned Jake.

'I hope your secretary isn't married,' she muttered.

'I don't have one; up to now I've never been in one place long enough. I dictate most of what I want typed into a tape recorder. Otherwise I borrow someone else's secretary.'

'Yes,' mused Caitlin, sharp twinges of jealousy scouring through her body. 'I can imagine you would.'

'Jake!' The secretary was hovering in the doorway, looking helpless. 'You promised that you'd show me the computer in your study, so we could look at the figures.'

'Oh, yes,' he said, grinning, unable to prevent his eyes from flickering briefly down her body. 'The figures.' He turned to Caitlin and caught her glaring, his grin becoming even broader. 'The contract we spoke of is on my desk. Please sign both copies and leave one. I imagine you will be helping Brigit with the dinner. She said it would be a simple one. We'll eat at eight.'

'Of course,' she said calmly, her mind whirling. She had to pull herself together and start thinking ahead! Caitlin stared after his broad back and resisted the strong temptation to swear. First beds, now dinner! Her first day in her new job hadn't gone too well: Jake had made assumptions about inviting guests without telling her what he expected, and she had made the mistake of not checking. She must be much more efficient in future.

Feeling rather panicky, she slipped into the study and signed the contracts. The salary was better than she'd expected; if she stuck this out for a while, she could soon be independent and might be able to rent a cottage on the estate, instead of living in the same house as Jake.

She was about to leave and see about dinner, when she saw that Jake's own books had arrived and were stacked in neat piles on the floor. Curiously, she walked over to inspect the titles. It might give her some clue to his background.

Instead of clarifying Jake's personality, they added to its mystery. There were a few foreign dictionaries, the most interesting being those in Arabic and Russian. There was a collection of books on living in the wild—probably connected with this Survival School of his in Tunisia—

and books on subjects as diverse as law, geology, anthropology and psychology. Caitlin frowned at the number of titles on aggression. Was he trying to cure his own behaviour? With a final, puzzled look at a couple of books on terrorism, she left thoughtfully, her fears increased.

Of course, reading about a certain subject didn't mean that it became your occupation, she reasoned. Yet . . . The clink of plates in the kitchen brought Caitlin to the present. Whatever Jake Ferriter's ulterior motives for setting up business here, he and his guests were expecting dinner! She ran into the kitchen and found that Brigit had managed to persuade Cormac to fetch some trout from the lake. That was a start.

Jake and the secretary came in for dinner a little late, and Caitlin's eyes blazed to see that the woman was flushed and a little dishevelled. Well, she thought, he'd said he would find another woman for his bed and she ought to get used to the idea. He didn't waste much time.

She wished the awful gnawing sensation in her chest would go away. It would have helped if Jake hadn't worn a dinner-jacket. He looked incredibly sexy. Compared to the other men, he was in another league. Caitlin quietly devoured him; the glossy, slicked back hair, his dark, excitedly glowing eyes, the fresh, smooth skin, so deeply tanned. His features were strong and definite, rather like the man himself, she mused.

He was laughing now, throwing his head back in delight at something the secretary had said, and Caitlin felt left out, as if he'd deliberately excluded her from his confidence. She had to get over these ridiculous feelings! Perhaps she ought to go out with Cormac. Looking at Jake, eagerly speaking of the two ships of the Spanish Armada, wrecked off White Strand, she knew she couldn't contemplate the idea. Only Jake filled her with a fierce energy for life, the desire to spend every moment in his company. And, she thought miserably, her body longed for his touch, sang out to him, with no hope of fulfilment, not in the way she wanted, anyway.

The talk was noisy again and few noticed that she hardly ate her eggs mimosa, or that she left much of the rainbow trout on her plate. They were all listening to the lakes consultant, rhapsodising over the fish. But Caitlin had been watching the secretary surreptitiously from under her lashes and seeing how she kept placing her hand on the cloth next to Jake's so that they touched.

Then something alerted Caitlin and she slanted her almond eyes in his direction. He was regarding her steadily with an inscrutable expression. How long he'd been observing her she didn't know; he simply gave her a slight smile and turned his attention back to the conversation.

For the next few days, Caitlin worked hard at playing the efficient and charming hostess, wanting Jake to think well of her, wanting to prove to him that she wasn't as useless as he imagined. Caitlin expected to miss the visitors when they left, because life had been so interesting, organising the house and supplies and listening to progress reports with Jake over dinner each evening. But Cashelkerry was immediately filled with architects and designers, engineers and inspectors. Work began on extending the lake and renovating the house, and her time was filled with discussions and decisions.

It was a joy to wake each morning with the prospect of so much to do, and she put aside the past and enjoyed every moment of the present. Cormac rarely made an appearance—Jake seemed to keep him so busy on the land and, according to Brigit, if Caitlin went off to Dingle town, that was the time Jake chose to call Cormac to the house.

Brigit found that very amusing, but Caitlin was upset that Jake should work so hard to keep them apart. She chatted to Cormac on the phone once or twice, but he was very cool. She wanted to say that she was only living in the same house as Jake, not living *with* him, but there wasn't a suitable moment. He seemed very disapproving.

Then, one morning, she was in the kitchen, making her own breakfast since it was Brigit's day off, when she was startled to see Jake through the window, wearily walking to the back door. She flung it open and he looked up in exhaustion.

'Good heavens! Whatever have you been doing? Are you all right?' she cried, helping him in.

He sank into a chair and stretched out his legs. 'That's better,' he grunted. 'Of course I'm all right.'

She examined his crumpled track-suit, his unshaven face, dark with stubble, and his tangled hair. He looked even more desirable than before. Tousled, rumpled and tired, Jake Ferriter still exuded a potent sexuality that stirred Caitlin's senses.

Then she realised he'd probably not spent the night in his own bed. 'You look like you've had a good night out,' she said icily.

'I have,' he agreed. 'Don't act the disapproving wife with me, Caitlin. I'm a grown man and can take care of myself.'

'Looks as if you didn't have to bother,' she snapped, going back to buttering a hot croissant.

'Hell, that smells good. Can I have some?'

Biting back the retort that he looked as if he'd had quite enough, she pushed the plate over and buttered another.

'Is that a green light I see in your eyes?' he murmured.

'No,' she answered, flicking back her hair. 'Green lights mean "go" and I doubt you've any energy left.'

'Oh, I don't know.' He grinned wolfishly. 'Why don't we see if I can rev up?'

'You're disgusting,' she said calmly, and stalked out.

'Hey, Caitlin! I've only been night climbing!' he yelled after her.

Night climbing! As if she believed that! He would have been carrying ropes and metal pins and things. And if he had been out all night on some innocent exercise he would have worn an anorak and had a sleeping-bag. He must think she was born yesterday!

For the rest of the morning she avoided him, leaving soup and snacks in the kitchen for Jake's lunch and taking a hot flask and sandwiches up to Ferriter's Crag. There she sat furiously planning her purchases for Cashel House and trying to keep her mind off its lusty master and his nocturnal wanderings. Living with him was becoming more and more difficult. At some stage she'd have to choose between torturing herself by being around to see his promiscuity and not being near him at all. He obviously took after his mother; their morals were the same. She stared gloomily at the misty horizon.

Later, a small, dark speck appeared in the pale grey sea. Someone had launched a currach and motored past the promontory rocks. Caitlin leant forwards, trying to make out the size and shape of the man in the little boat. It was almost certainly Jake! She bit her lip anxiously as he headed for the Strait. She shouted into the wind, but it caught her words of warning and threw them back mockingly into her face.

'Oh, no!' she whispered. 'Come back, come back! It's not safe! Not you, Jake, please, please, not you!'

Alone on the high promontory, she watched in horror as the little craft bobbed about in the treacherous current. She couldn't bear to watch and she couldn't bear not to.

'*Jake!*' she yelled, knowing it was fruitless, but desperate to will him to look up. 'Jake, don't,' she muttered miserably. 'Don't let him drown. Please don't let him drown,' she chanted, like a litany.

He had changed her life, she thought with a sob. He'd given it meaning. Everything she did was focused on him, it was all for him, it...

Caitlin closed her eyes as the full knowledge of her feelings hit her as if she'd run into a solid wall. He meant everything to her. With him, life was sweet and promising. Her fears for him now weren't connected with dreading a repeat of Mother's and Patrick's drowning, nor a mere wish that a human being should not perish before her eyes.

Her pain was utterly selfish; she wanted him to live so that she could be alive too. And then, as she examined her feelings, she realised that it was more than that. She didn't even care if Jake Ferriter never glanced her way; if only he lived, that would be enough.

Her lids shot open again and she stood helplessly watching, the skirts of her red wool dress plastered against her legs by the strong wind and her hair blowing across her face in long, stinging strands. She was looking at the man she loved.

'Oh, Jake,' she whispered. 'You could have been my world.'

And yet he treated her as he treated all women—as a casual pleasure. She'd stupidly fallen in love with a fascinating libertine who was about to disappear from her life for ever.

The figure in the currach waved and Caitlin held her breath at his ignorance of the danger. She tried to signal to him, but the tiny, faraway arm dropped and then, confidently and surely, the boat was manoeuvred into the safe channel and was heading towards Brandon Island.

Caitlin stared, unbelieving, absolutely furious. He handled the boat like an expert! Brilliantly, he'd accurately gauged the presence of the channel and given her all that distress for nothing! Strong feelings had surfaced to plague and haunt her, all for nothing! An unreasonable anger flooded through her. He ought to have remembered that she'd watched two people she loved drown! Then she grudgingly recalled that, in her note she'd left, she'd said she was possibly going to shop in Dingle. Jake didn't know she was going to be on the Crag.

He didn't return for dinner that evening. She ate alone, finding it quiet and boring without him. It was a black night, dark clouds obscuring the moon and stars. Caitlin paced up and down, worrying, wondering and cursing him in turn. She didn't want to have these feelings about him, she didn't want to be more vulnerable than ever. He had all the aces. Everything he wanted just fell into his lap, and she was darned if she would too!

If she once let him know that his escapades worried her, he'd move in and begin his sensual seduction all over again. Jake was so ruthless that she wasn't sure how far she could trust him—how much he would hold back if she admitted that she wanted him but couldn't contemplate an affair. She'd seen the way he worked with other people. When confronted with opposition, he went silent and, in a deceptively casual way, continued to bide his time until an opportunity came to reinstate his wishes. Calmly, never deviating from his chosen path, he got his own way.

And that was with people who had to be won over to his side! She was already there, what chance did she have?

In the darkness, far out to sea, something glowed. Caitlin's forehead creased as she made a calculation. It must be a fire, on the island. Stiff and cold, she stayed by the huge windows in the drawing-room till well after the heating went off for the night. The red glow had gone. She rose, intending to go to bed, when she saw another light and this time it was moving. It seemed to be coming nearer to shore and the light flickered with long, licking flames.

With a groan, Caitlin ran into the lobby and pulled on her boots and a thick sheepskin, huddling into its fleecy warmth as the cold night air bit into her face. She drew her torch from her pocket and followed the path down to the jetty, her heart in her mouth. Jake's boat must be on fire!

She stumbled along, trying to look where she was going and keep an eye on the red glow at the same time, trying not to let herself get in a state. Jake might need her help, she might have to launch a currach herself into that black, windy sea, and help him to reach the shore. She glanced up frantically, searching the dark expanse of water. The light had gone. There was nothing out in the bay, nothing!

With a wild, despairing cry, Caitlin ran down the path to the jetty, intent only on putting out to sea so that she could pluck Jake from the water. Nothing mattered but that, not even her own safety. Tears were running down her face and she was sobbing, her breath coming fitfully.

Then she bumped straight into someone, a hard body, dark and menacing, the torch dropping to the ground, and she was screaming at him, tearing at his body with her nails, refusing to accept that this prowler might stop her from finding Jake.

Her head reeled from a stinging slap and she widened her eyes in shock, her whole body rigid.

'Caitlin! Oh, Caitlin, what is it?'

'Jake!' She drew back, a hysterical delight flooding through her as she peered at the indistinct face.

'What the hell are you doing?' he asked.

'You devil!' she spat. 'You—you...'

'Gently, Caitlin. Calm down. I'm sorry if I gave you a shock, and I apologise for slapping you, but you went mad! Why are you here at this time of night?'

Caitlin's legs gave way and she sank to the grass in relief. He was safe and alive, and she had been worried out of her mind for no reason at all!

'Damn you, Jake Ferriter!' she grated through clenched teeth.

'Well, thanks,' he drawled. 'Why especially now?'

'You might let me know what you're up to,' she said shakily. 'I saw you in the Strait and worried that you might drown.'

'I know, I waved so that you'd be reassured,' he said gently. 'Caitlin, I'm going to be sailing over to the island, sometimes alone, sometimes with people on the course. You'll need to get used to that. I appreciate the fact that it brings back memories when you see people out there, but I want to use the island.'

'No!' she breathed, her eyes gleaming in the dark. 'It's a special place. I don't want people on it.'

'We'd better discuss this in the morning,' he said, and Caitlin recognised the steely determination in his tone. He was hell-bent on getting his own way again!

'We'll discuss it now,' she said obstinately.

'Caitlin, it's late and I'm tired. And in any case, weren't you going somewhere?'

'Of course I wasn't,' she said impatiently. 'I was worried about you.'

'I don't think so. Wasn't that earlier, when you saw me in the Strait going to the island? What made you come out at this hour?'

'I—I happened to be looking out of the window. I saw a light in the sea. It looked as though your currach was on fire,' she said. 'And then...' She stifled a sob. 'Then the light disappeared.'

'Oh, that,' said Jake casually. 'I was fishing.'

'*Fishing?*' she repeated.

'I took a bucket of peat with me and lit it. The fish are attracted and it keeps me warm. It's an old trick,' he said. 'When I'd caught a few fish, I dunked the bucket in the sea and made for home.'

'You...you...oh!' Caitlin was incapable of speech and sprang to her feet. Then she was almost blinded by the bright glare of torchlight.

'Cait?' muttered Jake uncertainly. 'You've been crying.'

'No, I *haven't*,' she denied, dashing her knuckles against her wet cheeks and betraying herself completely.

Jake's chuckle infuriated her still further and she whirled around, intending to flee from his mockery, knowing that somehow she had to stop him from knowing she'd been crying for his sake. Jake, of course, as she ought to have known, was too quick for her, and she was in his arms before she could go more than a few steps.

His fingers traced the tears on her face by feel alone, the torch discarded. Jake soothed her, gentled her, till her tense, tautly strung body relaxed and she rested her head on his shoulder.

'You could have been killed,' she whispered into his warm neck. 'The weather might have prevented you from returning, or the sea might have got up in this wind...'

'No,' he answered. 'You must trust my judgement, Caitlin, or you'll be worrying unnecessarily all the time. I didn't tell you where I was going today because I wanted to try the trip out for myself without you knowing. In future I will keep you informed about my movements. Well,' he said, with a small laugh, 'most of them.'

Caitlin tensed again. 'It's just that it's necessary for the business,' she said stiffly, trying to pull away. She stood in the circle of his arms, looking at him from under angry brows. 'I need to know where you are.'

'Yes, I know. Now, look, I don't take stupid risks. Life is too precious to me for that. Every time I do something like this I have a detailed weather report and check on the tides. I work out the odds before I go. I'm perfectly safe. Does that make you happier?'

'I wasn't worried about *you*,' she lied, trying not to let her lips tremble. Caitlin hated to lie, but she'd be in Jake Ferriter's bed if she didn't! He'd know that she wouldn't cry unless she was emotionally entangled. 'It was the memories. I couldn't bear the same accident to happen again.'

'No,' he said gently. 'Of course not.'

'You do understand, don't you?' she asked with an attempt at haughtiness.

'I understand,' he said softly.

CHAPTER SIX

To Caitlin's relief, he did understand. He'd apologised again and politely walked back with her, promising to keep her fully informed in future. In the weeks that followed, he treated her with a cautious courtesy, as if he knew he was skating on thin ice. All the time it seemed he was remembering the tragedies of her life and didn't want to touch on a raw nerve.

But it meant that he held his enthusiasm in check, and was more restrained when she was around. Caitlin longed for him to let go and speak to her in the same way he did to everyone else. She saw other people flare to life in the full blast of his vital energy, and resented that there was none for her.

Still, there were compensations. Cashel House and the demesne were filled with a small army of workers, some living in temporary field huts beyond the woods. There was a mix of Jake's men and local experts and labourers, so he was very popular with everyone for creating so much employment.

It was mid-November, a dry day after much rain, and Jake had discovered that both he and Caitlin were bound for the small town of Dingle. He'd suggested they shared his car and she was waiting for him in the hall.

Every day she admired it, glad that Cashel House was being restored to its former glory. The chandeliers glinted after their thorough cleaning; the walls looked beautiful in the apricot damask that she had chosen. She stood on one of the huge white cotton rugs which softened the black and white flagstones, happy to spend the day with Jake and telling herself just to enjoy it and not to get wistful about him!

Her heart missed a beat when he came down the stairs and she kicked herself mentally. Like her, he wore casual cords, a jumper and shirt. Unlike her, she sighed, sexuality oozed from every pore.

With a cool smile, she spun on her heel and walked out to his car.

'If you don't mind, Caitlin,' he said, 'I'd like to drive.'

She shrugged. 'As you please.'

'Marvellous day, isn't it?' he said pleasantly, as the car moved smoothly away.

She smiled non-committally, trying to settle herself into a semblance of normality. It was a lovely day. Everything had that intense clarity that came after rain. In the gentle, fresh breeze, her hair blew back in a dark stream from her carefully poised head.

'I thought the view would be perfect today,' he continued, turning off on to a narrow track.

'Wrong way,' she said, surprised that he should make a mistake. 'Dingle is straight on.'

'This is the quick route,' came the laconic answer. 'Through the pass.'

'You meant to come down here? Have you ever been on this road?' she cried, sitting up erect.

'Frequently.' He grinned. 'Have you?'

'Once,' she breathed. 'And never again. It's very narrow. There's a terrible, long drop all the way down the mountainside and no barrier. Hardly anyone uses this road. Turn back!'

'It's the fastest route,' he repeated.

'The most dangerous,' she said in a small voice, understanding him a little more. He lived for danger. 'And you really intend to risk my life for your own selfish excitement?'

'Fear not, gentle maiden,' he mocked. 'I'm a damn good driver. You're in safe hands.'

She gave an exasperated sniff and fell silent, concentrating on the road on his behalf, as they continued to climb higher and higher, driving quite fast as he took the hairpin bends which swung out into terrifying drops. Each time they hurtled towards the edge, Caitlin gripped the edge of her seat, fear mingling with a tug of excitement in her breast. Each time Jake judged the road with expertise, enjoying the challenge of manoeuvring the responsive car.

They were above the tree-line and roaring around a series of corries, their curving sides dropping to deep black tarns, silently and mysteriously mirroring the mountains and sky above. The air was chilly, biting into Caitlin's face, stinging her cheeks a rosy red. She began to revel in the thrilling drive and the sensation of wind cleansing her body. They topped the pass to a blast of invigorating air and he stopped the car.

'Come on,' he said eagerly. 'Let's look at the view.'

'You can't leave the car in the middle of the road!' she objected.

He raised a laughing eyebrow and moved around to open the door for her. 'You don't imagine that anyone would be fool enough to come up here, do you?' he asked innocently.

Caitlin pressed her lips together in exasperation, leaping out without thinking. Her legs were shaking more than she thought and she had to clutch at him for a moment. The pressure of his hands was light and courteous, but drove deeply into her very being. They were motionless for a second or two, while Jake waited for her to steady herself and Caitlin tried not to acknowledge the fire that flared within her.

'Bit wobbly,' she laughed nervously.

'Yes. Me too,' he agreed. 'From the drive.'

'Yes.'

'Shall we climb to the summit? It's not far and the view is worth it,' he said quietly.

She nodded and they made their way up the gently rising slope. The Dingle peninsula lay before them, green and clear in the clean air. Islands lay like broken beads from a necklace in the sparkling sea which rolled its white edges on to half-moon shaped sandy bays.

Behind them lay a different scene, wild mountains and valleys, reflected in the limpid water of the lakes scoured by glaciers. The silence was broken only by the silent boom of a waterfall which fell in an awesome cataract of smooth, molten lead over a precipice in one glistening sheet of water, crashing in a seething, foaming cloud into a black pool.

In mutual agreement, they sat on the crag and dreamed their own dreams, disturbed only by the powerful wind.

Caitlin thought of the companionship that Jake could give to her. From deep inside her had come a grudging pleasure in his company. His offer of a different kind of relationship grew more and more tempting. Yet her morality and self-respect denied her the courage to take a chance on getting involved with him. She didn't have the confidence to believe that she could be the woman who made him change his mind about marriage. If she behaved like all other women, and gave in to him, she would not only lose her own regard, but his as well.

'I'm cold,' she complained, unable to sit beside him any longer in such intimate solitude.

Her manner was distant—so distant that he didn't put his arm around her as a casual friend might, in order to warm her up, even though every fibre of her being was willing him to. They returned to the car.

Jake shifted around in his seat to look at her, and didn't start the engine as she'd expected. 'Do you think we'll ever find peace of mind, Caitlin?' he asked unexpectedly.

'Not the way you're living,' she said sourly.

'No,' he agreed in a sober tone. 'But I'm working on it. Rather more slowly than I'd planned, however.'

'That doesn't sound like you,' she commented.

He gave a rueful laugh. 'It doesn't, does it? Maybe I ought to speed things up a little.'

Jake reached over and pushed back the wisps of hair from her face, his fingers lingering alarmingly on the nape of her neck. Caitlin flinched and drew back, her body stiff and unwelcoming, but her beautiful brown eyes were as startled as a deer and her lips parted in need.

'You have a pure and virginal mind and a wicked, sinful body, Caitlin O'Connell,' he murmured.

'You said you wouldn't make improper suggestions!' she gasped.

'I'm not,' he drawled. 'I'm stating the facts.'

To her dismay, he edged nearer, his arm resting casually along the back of the seat. She stared ahead, her pulses quickening, wondering how long she could keep a cool façade. He did nothing, apart from watching her, and it was as if something was willing her to turn her head to return his gaze. She was unnerved by his confidence and infuriated at the way he sat there, arrogantly waiting for her to fling herself at him.

'You have sex on the brain,' she scorned. 'There's nothing sinful about me, so stop imagining things. I am completely indifferent to you.'

'Point one,' he said, with a satisfied twist to his lips, 'if you think I have sex on the brain, you need a lesson in biology. Point two, you encourage sin by your mere presence, by the way you move. Point three, you are definitely not indifferent.'

'I am,' she said angrily.

'Then the next few minutes will do everything to release my pent-up hunger, and nothing to disturb you,' he snapped.

Before she knew what was happening, she was in his arms and his face was a hair's breadth away. Caitlin pushed against his hard chest to no avail and then tried to raise her hand to push at his face. But he forestalled her.

'I can play rougher than you,' he said menacingly, his eyes a hypnotically intense green. 'I've had more practice.'

Holding her prisoner against his body, he freed one hand but, instead of hurting her roughly as she half expected, he trailed his fingers along her cheekbone with such a light, feathering touch, that she almost strained to meet it.

'Must you inflict yourself on me? I don't like...' Her voice quavered.

He had traced the outline of her lips as she spoke, his own mouth parting like hers. A warm wash of feeling erupted within her and she tried to think of her shopping list for the groceries she intended to buy in town. She frowned, incapable of remembering any item at all.

Jake's big, warm hand curved around her breast, testing its weight and, as Caitlin sat there rooted to the spot, her limbs paralysed by longing, his hand swept over its peak, backwards and forwards, in a mind-numbing rhythm, but one which had a startling effect on her body.

A quiver ran right through her and she tried to stay on the straight and narrow path. Apples. She needed those. And... Oh, lord! He was gently squeezing her thrusting nipple through the soft material of her jumper, sending unbelievable spasms of pleasure searing throughout her body.

'Don't! I really must plan my shopping. The victualler,' she muttered aloud in desperation. 'For some lamb chops and... oh! And...'

Jake laughed softly. 'Give up, Caitlin.'

'Take your hands off me,' she said, trying to free her arms.

'Enjoy the pleasure we're both experiencing,' he said huskily, watching her from under hooded lids.

'Lamb chops,' she repeated, her voice rising. 'Then into the chemist for some... shampoo... oh! Look, I'm trying to... oh! *No*, Jake!' she said urgently, as his hand slid down her hips.

His grin infuriated her and she gritted her teeth against the deep throb of her loins. Jake's lips met hers, finding them hard and unyielding. He wriggled slightly, so that his knee pressed in shocking accuracy, parting her thighs and nudging firmly against her heat. It took all her will-power not to arch in a welcome to him, so urgent was her need to relieve the powerful beat of desire.

Too late, she discovered that in concentrating on his invading knee, her mouth had softened and he was already taking advantage of it, softly and moistly kissing her treacherous lips which responded with a shocking eagerness.

Then he was opening her mouth with his and the first dart of his probing tongue coincided with a gentle movement of his knee and Caitlin let out a deep groan from far inside her. Abandoning all pretence, she pressed against him, finding that he no longer imprisoned her arms and she joyfully reached up to wrap them around his neck. Willingly she connived in the seduction of her mouth by forcing his head down hard so that the pressure on her lips was increased.

Gently, slowly, he eased away, reluctance in his face.

'That's a remarkable show of indifference,' he teased softly.

But, despite the tenderness of his tone, it didn't alter the fact that Caitlin had betrayed herself. Miserable at how easy she'd been, she opened the car door and stalked off a little way, gazing down at the black Kerry cattle on the valley slopes far below.

'Cait?'

She swung around. 'If we weren't so far from town, I'd darn well walk!' she cried shakily.

Jake passed a hand over his hair. 'I'll drive you to Dingle. Get in. I won't touch you.'

'You think I trust you? A man who forces himself on——'

'Relax. It was only a kiss, wasn't it?' he said, angling his head at her enquiringly.

'A little more than that.'

'Get in, Caitlin,' he said gently. 'We'd better get those lamb chops before the shop closes.'

'It's all a game to you, isn't it?' she declared heatedly. 'An amusing masculine game where you can prove your virility and dominance over women!'

'Nothing of the kind,' he said quietly. 'I'm following my instincts. You ought to listen to yours a bit more.'

'And act the rake, like you?' she scorned.

'Wanting to kiss you is hardly acting like a rake.'

'What about that secretary? And those nights you stay out?' she accused.

'What secretary?' He frowned.

'The blonde with the long, long legs,' she snapped. 'You both came down late for dinner the first evening she arrived.'

His mouth twitched. 'So we did. I'd been showing her around outside. She asked me to. And you know that I need to get used to moving about at night.'

'Oh, yes,' she said scathingly. 'I remember. I think you're an expert in night manoeuvres. Apart from showing secretaries around, you climb cliffs without ropes in the pitch dark.'

'Of course I use ropes. What do you think I keep in the equipment shed? It's stacked full of all-weather gear and tackle. Go and look. Caitlin, when will you trust me?' he sighed.

'When your sex drive diminishes,' she said coolly.

He laughed ruefully. 'That long? Ah, well. I'll have to live with your suspicious mind. Come on, I have business in town.'

Reluctantly she slid into the passenger seat. Once in Dingle, they arranged to meet by Doyle's Seafood Bar and Caitlin marched off to do her shopping. Afterwards, she sat on a low wall waiting for Jake. She saw him approaching before he noticed her, and for a moment she was free to let herself yearn for him. Then his head moved in her direction and she pretended to be watching the passers-by.

'I'd like to sample a pub before we go, if you don't mind,' he said.

'OK,' answered Caitlin casually. She needed a drink to steady her nerves for the drive back.

'Where do you suggest? I saw that the grocer back there has a bar.'

'I prefer the dressmakers, they have better fires,' she said. 'Or the cobbler.'

'Fires?' he grinned. 'Well, whichever is nearest.'

They ducked their heads under the low lintel of O'Flaherty's the cobbler, elbowing aside bits of leather and shoe black on the counter. The Guinness was pulled with due ceremony and they waited for the cloudy chocolate liquid to clear. As soon as the glass turned black and the head became creamy, they each lifted their glasses and took a satisfying gulp.

''Tis a grand day,' said a man next to Jake.

'Marvellous. Like every day here.'

Caitlin glanced at him in surprise at his friendly tone and sipped her drink. He wanted something.

'Aye. 'Twill be wet later, I'm t'inkin'.'

'Do you think so?' Jake frowned.

'Sure, 'n there'll be a terrible gale come the next night. The wind'll be whipping the sea up to the sky like it was a great big curtain, and all the little boats will be blown up there like they was little black birds.'

Jake laughed and the man laid a hand on his arm.

'Don't think it's a lie I'm tellin'. Aren't all the signs laid out for the reading?' continued the man.

Caitlin smiled to herself as Jake questioned him, apparently fascinated by his weather lore. They exchanged telephone numbers and she was disconcerted by his immediate friendship with the man, who tipped his cap to Caitlin and then left.

She and Jake stared at the colours in the turf flames and he sniffed appreciatively at the sweet, lingering scent from the past. An old man reached down a fiddle, tested the strings, then began to play a jig, the breathless, fast music making her feet tap.

That evening was one of the most enjoyable Caitlin had ever spent. They didn't do anything in particular, just sat on the high stools, thoughtfully provided with a back as a safeguard against instant paralysis from the now-illegal home-made poteen, a pint of which, promised Caitlin, was powerful enough to immobilise any normal man.

They chatted about nothing of importance, and drifted into conversation with the friendly people, Jake especially delighting in the soft accents and elaborate, dramatic way of speaking. She wanted her life to consist of moments like this: Jake's friendship, a home at Cashel and an interesting job. Ought she to expect anything more? Her eyes fell to Jake's bared arm resting on the counter, his fist contentedly wrapped around his glass. One of the men rose to join in the impromptu jig and his elbow knocked a jug of ale on the counter. With incredibly fast reactions, Jake caught the jug before it fell to the floor. Caitlin's eyes grew serious. He'd reacted almost automatically, far quicker than any businessman might, however much he exercised, however much he'd become involved in the outdoor life.

He moved and behaved like a trained professional. Was he keeping something from her? Was there more to Jake Ferriter than he gave out? The books on terrorism loomed up in her mind. She frowned, wondering about his prison sentence. She'd forgotten that. And, however relaxed he might appear, his quick reaction in catching the jug had proved that he was, in fact, constantly alert. It would be as well for her to remember that.

'Shall we leave?' she suggested quietly. 'The lamb chops need to get into a fridge soon.'

'So you did buy some.' He grinned.

Caitlin's dark brows made a fierce line.

'Sorry!' Jake laughed.

The drive back, towards the setting sun, was a silent one. Red dappled clouds raced in a rolling blanket over the sky, casting sinister shadows on the hills. As the light went, a thin vapour rose from the ground, giving the scene an unearthly silken sheen.

'Look, Caitlin, Bewick's swans,' cried Jake in delight, pointing.

To her, they were just swans, stretching out their long necks as they flapped gracefully towards Cashelkerry.

'I know some lovely folk tales about swans,' she mused.

'Oh, good. I like bedtime stories,' said Jake enthusiastically.

She had to laugh. 'Don't you ever let up?' she complained.

'No.' He grinned, his white teeth flashing in the darkness. 'And aren't you glad?'

Caitlin laughed with him and shook her head in mock exasperation. Then they rounded the headland which jutted out into the sea and Jake slammed on his brakes hard, flinging out an arm to protect her. A huge white launch lay at anchor, some distance from the shore, and Jake's ferocious glare was directed there.

Then his lashes dropped. 'Sorry,' he said. 'My foot slipped. Nice boat, isn't it?'

Grimly he accelerated away, his body tense. Caitlin wondered why he'd lied and why the boat should bother him so much.

'You haven't told me everything about yourself, have you?' she began, unable to bear the stony silence.

'No,' he said shortly. 'Have you?'

She flushed and kept quiet. If he didn't trust her, it was no wonder that she didn't trust him!

When they arrived at Cashel House, he went straight to his study, shutting the door firmly and leaving Caitlin to put away the shopping herself, instead of helping her with the heavier items. The phone in the kitchen clicked as he dialled and he seemed to be talking for a long time. He'd already told her that he wouldn't be eating dinner with her, and he left soon after.

By midnight, he hadn't returned and Caitlin decided to turn off the television and go to bed. In the ensuing silence she heard a dog barking. It was probably Danny, as he was the only dog around now. Maybe he was rounding up Jake, she thought with a smile.

The barking became frantic. Caitlin paused in the act of turning off the lights downstairs. There came a spine-chilling howl. She ran to a window and stared out at the darkness. The wind was stronger; the man in

O'Flaherty's shop was right, the weather was breaking up again.

Because of the way the wind was blowing, Danny's barking wouldn't be heard by anyone else; she was the only living person in this direction. From the frantic howls, Danny had got into some kind of trouble. She knew the land well enough, and could find him by the noise he was making. She wasted no more time, but pulled on a stormcoat and her boots and set off into the darkness.

The wind grabbed at her, and she stumbled. The sound came from Ferriter's Crag and the wind was doing its best to hold her back, the light from her torch bobbing about as she staggered in the increasing gale. Just below the crest of the crag, the sound of barking intensified. It seemed to be coming from her feet!

Astonished, she shone her torch directly down on to the huge slabs of stone that made a kind of path up to the castle. There was a scrabbling sound a little further up and Danny's white and black face appeared from a dark hole, then his body. Caitlin was just about to go to him, when he shot off into the darkness. Before she could swing the beam of her torch away, she saw a shaking hand grip the edge of the same hole, then Jake's white face.

'Not you again!' he growled. 'Put that damn light out. I can't see.'

There was something odd about his voice. To Caitlin, it sounded uneven. She moved nearer.

'Good heavens! It's a souterrain!' she exclaimed in surprise.

'What?' Jake heaved himself out and sat panting slightly with exertion.

'An underground escape tunnel, from the old Iron Age fort. They're very common. If it looked likely that the fort would be captured, the inhabitants slipped away under the feet of their attackers and emerged behind them.'

'Smart people.'

'I never knew it existed. This just seemed like an over-grown path. I suppose the exit is blocked up further down the hill. Did Danny fall down the hole? The rain must have made the stones unstable, and opened up a crack.'

'He fell down and couldn't get up again,' grunted Jake, not making a move despite the howling wind. 'I'd been down to the bay and was returning when I heard him. He'd gone about twenty yards down the tunnel. It's dangerous—we'll have to mark it off.'

Caitlin glanced out to sea. The launch was now moored to the jetty. What had he been doing? Then she thought about Jake clambering into what might have been a bottomless well, or a disused copper mine, and shivered. He'd risked his life for a dog. Her eyes glowed.

'It must have been an unnerving experience, lowering yourself into the souterrain,' she said earnestly.

'Very.'

Either he was suffering from the exhaustion of hauling himself some distance underground, with a dog in his arms, or he was trying to pass off the rescue in an attempt at modesty. He certainly wasn't encouraging discussion!

'Poor old Danny! Murphy will be grateful. I think you were very brave.'

'Come on,' he said abruptly. 'We'll get chilled up here.'

Thoughtfully, Caitlin followed his broad back. In the torchlight, she saw that his clothes were filthy with mud and her heart somersaulted at his dejected figure. A longing to take him in her arms swept over her. For once in his life, Jake seemed vulnerable, as though he needed someone—really needed them, not merely to sate his desire for sex.

'Jake,' she said, quickening her step and bobbing alongside him, 'is there anything I can do for you?'

His eyes slanted cynically to hers and then away, his mouth working. 'No,' he replied brusquely. 'Leave me alone, Caitlin. I'll explain some other time.'

'Explain what?' she asked, hurt that he didn't want her help.

'Leave it!' he snapped, his face forbidding.

Caitlin felt a lump rise in her throat. So now she knew where she really stood. He was interested in her superficially, as a woman to dispense tea and cocktails and as a feminine enhancement to his dinner-table. He was also prepared to take her to bed, providing, presumably, she didn't expect any other involvement in his secret, private life. Other than that, she was nothing to him. Absolutely dispensable. It wasn't a pleasant feeling, knowing that a few million other women could be what she was to Jake Ferriter.

As she pretended to push her hair away from her eyes, and in fact was furtively brushing away tell-tale tears, she saw the lights on the white launch go out. All right, if their relationship was to be businesslike, then she ought to know what was going on.

'Are the men in the boat friends of yours?' she asked coldly.

'That's right.'

'Will we be entertaining them?'

'No.'

'Why are they there?'

'Personal reasons. Nothing to do with Cashelkerry. They'll be gone tomorrow.'

Her mouth formed a tight line. There was something odd going on and she didn't like it, but she couldn't force him to confide in her. She was beginning to think that she had to get away, that she mustn't get involved, however innocent she was of his mysterious past and the equally secretive present.

They returned to the house and she noticed how white he still looked and that his hands still trembled slightly. He went straight up to his room, and the water system, as yet not improved, gurgled and rumbled as he took what seemed to be an unending shower.

The next morning she picked up the kitchen phone to check on an order for ceiling mouldings, and found that Jake was dialling from the study. She bit her lip and slowly began to lower the receiver, only to hear him speaking to Cormac.

'Collect a Rolls from Dingle Car Hire,' Jake ordered. 'Be at White Strand in two hours. I'll meet you there and introduce you to some friends of mine who want to go to Dublin. I'd like you to drive them there. Do you speak French?'

'Er—no, I don't,' said Cormac.

'Just as well,' he said cryptically. 'They don't speak English at all. They're Muslims, so don't suggest a pub lunch. Treat them well, Cormac, they're special. Drop them at the airport and find somewhere to stay overnight.'

'Right, sir,' agreed Cormac, plainly pleased at the prospect of a luxurious hotel.

The phone clicked, and Caitlin replaced her receiver. That must be the people from the boat. It was interesting that he hadn't arranged for them to be picked up at the house, which would have been more civilised. White Strand beach was isolated, of course, and away from prying eyes. Jake was being secretive again. His friends couldn't bring the motor launch into White Strand bay, because of the currents, so they'd have to walk over the beach path.

Caitlin had an idea. She pulled on a warm jersey that reached way down over her hips, and the snug stretch cords, and fetched her beachcaster. She'd go down to the beach and pretend to fish. He couldn't help but introduce her. Then she realised that wouldn't get her very far, if they didn't speak English! Her French was hardly up to conversations. Even better, she could slip into the small cave. That would give her a good opportunity to discover what Jake was up to. The paths from Smugglers' Cove and the house met just above the cave.

Her hand gripped the fishing-rod nervously. In a strange way she didn't want to know anything bad about Jake. But it would be better to hear the worst, rather than imagine all kinds of things about him. Last night, she had almost decided he was a mercenary. That would fit in with being in Angola. But he couldn't be a successful businessman as well!

She began to run, intent on reaching the cave before he left the house. What she was doing might be dangerous if he was mixed up in something shady. She thought of his physical strength and his unyielding grip and shivered.

CHAPTER SEVEN

IT MUST have rained in the early hours of the morning because the ground was quite wet. Caitlin wondered whether there was time for her to go back to the house and fetch her stormcoat, but decided against it. The sky looked clear enough, and she could always make a dash for home if rainclouds appeared. She came to the end of the path and contemplated the beach. Jake was bound to notice if she walked over it to the cave. A wry smile curved her mouth. Now she too was beginning to think secretively!

Her short boots sank a little in the muddy ground as she stood, thinking, and she wondered if he'd notice that too, then dismissed the idea. He wasn't Superman. She scuffed at the grass a little, hoping it would spring back eventually, and walked as lightly as she could to a gorse bush, feeling that she was being overcautious.

Nevertheless, she broke off a few gorse branches, and trod carefully over the beach, dragging the branches behind her.

It seemed a long wait. Caitlin quickly grew cold and bored. This wasn't such a good idea, after all! It seemed a lot of effort—too much—to find out who Jake was meeting. After all, Cormac could probably tell her about the men. Still, she'd been hoping for some kind of clue in what they said to Jake, and even though her French was minimal she might recognise one or two significant words.

It had been worth a try, she told herself, half inclined to leave. Darn it! Surely... She glanced at her watch and groaned. The tide was on the turn. In an hour, the cave would be swirling with water!

Caitlin reached for the fishing-rod and then froze at the distant sound of voices. Grim-faced, she huddled back in the rock fissure. If she came out now, she'd have to use her wits to convince Jake that she'd been fishing— and suddenly she wasn't sure that she could lie convincingly enough. He had the unnerving ability to see right through her.

With growing concern, she eyed the water's edge. It wouldn't flood the cave, but might reach her knees, and that would be frightening enough in the enclosed space. What an idiot she was! And yet... how could she calm her suspicions and reassure herself that she could trust Jake, unless she did a little investigating of her own?

If she voiced her worries to him, she'd make a fool of herself if he was completely innocent of anything illegal. He'd be deeply offended to know it had even crossed her mind that he might be some kind of gangster, or evading the law in some way.

On the other hand, if he was up to no good, it was better if he didn't know she was snooping. Caitlin remembered his anger when he'd found that Cormac had searched the long-house—and that Jake admitted he knew of the search because of some precautions he'd taken. That wasn't the action of an innocent man. She had to stay in the cave, despite the oncoming tide. Misery swept over her.

Men's laughter, deep and booming and almost directly above her now, caused Caitlin to tense her body expectantly. They called Jake's name and she prepared to listen. But instead of speaking in French, as she'd expected, they had a long conversation in a guttural tongue, presumably Arabic. Darn it! All that subterfuge for nothing! The voices receded a little and she peered out cautiously.

There were four men in business suits, carrying hand grips. Two had their arms around Jake's shoulders in a friendly way, and two walked behind, scanning the countryside. As they turned in her direction, she dived for cover again, noticing that waves had begun to lap at the entrance.

Caitlin waited. After an interminable time, the sound of Cormac's car and cheerful farewells died away. She resigned herself to remaining forever in ignorance of Jake's real business interests. That left her with her emotional feelings, and she felt her spirits droop even more because their parting was looking more and more certain. She couldn't stay with him, harbouring the suspicions she did—and, being unwillingly attracted to him, nor could she bear to be merely another woman in his life.

That settled it. Today she'd give in her notice. Caitlin clenched her fists at the pains knifing through her body.

'You'd better come out,' came Jake's voice.

Caitlin jumped, rattled by his characteristically silent approach. But it was a second before his figure actually appeared at the mouth of the cave. How did he know she was there, before he even checked?

'Jake?' she called in pretended surprise. 'Is that you?' The figure might be lit from behind and therefore his features undistinguishable, but she knew Jake's body and the way he stood as if that had been carved into her brain. Quickly she waggled her fishing-rod for him to see. 'Hello! Are you fishing too?'

His expression was unreadable. 'No. I normally fix a reel to my rod when I fish,' he answered lazily.

'Oh!' She flushed, furious with herself. 'How stupid! It's a good thing I wasn't relying on the morning's catch for lunch,' she bluffed quickly.

'Nice try, Caitlin. Why don't we start levelling with each other, though? You start, by telling me why you were hiding in this cave.'

'Hiding? What makes you say that?'

'Because you took the trouble to leave the path to the beach, collect some branches and cover your tracks. That can't have been to keep your presence a secret from the fish, now can it?' he asked mildly.

Caitlin wasn't fooled by his offhand manner. He couldn't prevent his eyes from glittering in that rapacious, predatory manner, and she knew she was in trouble. He stood blocking the cave entrance, black and sinister in the grey light, the tide rising over his boots and creeping hungrily to her feet.

'How do you know that?' she asked nervously. 'Were you watching me?'

'No. I noticed the ground had been disturbed beside the path. The grass was bruised and there were white scars on the gorse bush where you'd torn away the branches. I could just make out where the sand had been smoothed.'

'Observant, aren't you?' she snapped.

'It's second nature to me. Besides, gorse branches don't normally stroll into caves.' He indicated the evidence, behind her.

'What made you so sure I was in here?' she asked crossly, wishing he hadn't found out and made her look stupid.

'I know every inch of this coastline now. It was the most obvious place,' he said scornfully, and Caitlin cringed. 'Why were you spying on me?'

'The tide's coming in!' she said, trying to avoid answering. He folded his arms and heaved a sigh of exasperation.

'Caitlin, I don't like being followed or spied on. It gives me an uncomfortable feeling.'

'I'm not afraid of you!' she lied, her eyes huge.

'I should damn well hope not!' he frowned. There was a moment's silence as he contemplated her thoughtfully. 'We really do have to talk. We can't go on living together as we are at the moment. You might be able to stand it, but I can't.'

'You want me to leave?' she asked tremulously.

'Hell, Caitlin, are you deliberately being obtuse?' he muttered. 'Look, I have an idea. I'm going over to the island. Why not come over for the ride? We can start to clear things up on the way. Then you won't have to creep about like this any more.'

'No, I don't think that's a good idea.'

'You could help me,' he coaxed. 'I discovered last time I went that some of my ancestors are buried there, and I want to write their names and dates down. Sentiment's sake, you know.'

She looked at him doubtfully, the idea of Jake Ferriter being sentimental rather preposterous, even though he'd made that claim before.

'I'm going in the launch,' he added.

'The big white one?' she asked in surprise.

'Yes. It belongs to me now. Don't you want to find out how?' he grinned.

'I don't trust you,' she muttered.

'That makes us quits.'

'You're the one who's behaving oddly——'

'You're the one who's sneaking around checking up on me,' he retaliated. 'You know you're innocent, I know I'm innocent, so why don't we share our clear consciences on the way to Brandon Island?'

'Why not at the house?' Caitlin glanced down at the incoming tide, eddying around her ankles.

'Don't look a gift horse in the mouth,' he said implacably. 'I'm offering to tell you everything about me. You can at least be generous enough to fit in with my busy schedule. I need to go over to the island this morning. It's a question of now or never. I'm in the mood to spill the beans about myself. If you refuse to come, I might not feel inclined to do so later.'

'That sounds rather like a mild form of blackmail,' she muttered.

'It is,' he smiled. 'I believe in taking all the opportunities that I can.'

Like graciously accepting what willing women have to offer, she thought irritably.

'The weather...' she began, not having seen the forecast, and vaguely remembering an earlier warning of storms.

'The weather is perfect. Couldn't be better,' he said earnestly.

Caitlin chewed her lip. Jake's eyes were pleading now. Intuitively she knew that he really did want to confide in her. Despite all the evidence, she was actually incapable of believing that he was evil. That might be, of

course, some kind of defence mechanism inside her, re-
fusing to think ill of the man she desired so illogically.
Yet... she wasn't the only one who'd fallen for Jake
Ferriter. Brigit, Cormac, the Murphys, all the people who
worked for him... People liked him a lot. And he'd saved
Danny.

'Don't you want to clear up everything between us?
To have an honest questions and answers session?' he
asked quietly.

He looked sincere, even a little anxious, as Caitlin
studied his eyes.

'All right,' she said grudgingly.

A gentle smile lit his face and she faltered as he helped
her out. They trudged over the path to Smugglers' Cove
and down to the jetty. Caitlin pulled off her boots and
climbed up the short ladder on to the deck.

'Flash, isn't it?' grinned Jake. 'Rather like a floating
gin palace!'

Her eyes travelled around the expensive teak decks and
the mass of chrome fittings. It must have cost a great
deal.

'Did the men sell it to you?'

'No, it was a gift.'

Her stomach hollowed. Corruption? Bribery? An
under-the-counter exchange for business put in the hands
of those on the beach? She moistened her mouth.

'For something you did?' she croaked.

Jake roared with laughter and flung an arm around
her shoulders, drawing her tight to him in a bear-like
hug. 'Stop imagining I'm a smuggler, or exporting
slaves!' he chuckled.

'Don't be ridiculous!' she said hotly. 'Just...a kind
of skilful playing of the business market...something
a bit unorthodox.'

He smiled to himself and went to cast off, directing
Caitlin to a high stool in the covered cockpit. After a
moment, he took the seat next to her.

The launch was luxurious inside and very spacious,
more like a small flat than a boat. Effortlessly it skimmed
the choppy waves, making the trip to the island brief.
Jake seemed very relaxed and exchanged easy smiles with
her as she opened drawers and lockers in front of her,
finding a drinks cabinet, a rack filled with yesterday's
papers, and a small fridge packed with beer. Apparently
that was only the drinks cabinet for the cockpit, and
there was a larger fridge below! Caitlin marvelled at the
comfort.

Jake still told her nothing confidential, though. Caitlin
studied his face, intending to ask a barrage of questions,
but she saw that his eyes were constantly scanning the
sea and she realised that the safe channel was as yet rela-
tively unknown to him and he needed all his concentration. Perhaps she could take the wheel on the way
back—or they might sit for a while on the island and
talk.

She began to feel confident in the way he handled the
boat, and enjoyed the trip. The rough water caught the
rays of the sun which made jewels of the spray from the
bows. The streamlined shape of a cormorant sped over
the sea in its long, low flight, and soon they could hear
the scream of thousands of sea birds as they neared the
black, forbidding cliffs of Brandon Island.

Jake made for the narrow fissure in the rock which
led to the island's sheltered harbour. Caitlin was sur-

prised that he took the boat right into the inner harbour. It hadn't been used since the last inhabitants left, twenty years ago. Even in rough weather it stayed like a mill-pond. Today it shone like a mirror, half blinding them with the brilliant reflection of the sun's rays.

There were plenty of fenders on the launch, but maybe Jake was being extra careful with his new boat. The sea certainly had been choppy by the outer jetty.

She went with Jake to the small graveyard by the ruined church, ten minutes' walk away, and did her best to curb her curiosity while he wandered around happily, discovering his ancestors' grave.

After a short while, his enthusiasm and delight made her tense suspicion recede. He could be so charming when he wanted, she mused, watching him eagerly writing down details from his great-grandfather's headstone. When he'd finished, he rose from his haunches and glanced quickly at the sky.

Caitlin froze. She'd been so inanely occupied with the way the wind was tugging at his hair, how his eyes crinkled up when he concentrated, and how much she wanted to touch the smooth back of his long, tanned hand, that she'd been totally unaware of the change in the weather!

They were in trouble. The sky had become a menacing yellow, above a long, dark and ominous line.

'Jake!' she cried urgently. 'There's a line-squall coming! We must get back to the mainland.'

'Too late. It's travelling fast,' he muttered. 'I can't risk it hitting us when we're crossing the Strait. We'd better head for the boat. We'll be safe enough there— it's very sheltered.'

Icy rain fell, long before they'd run very far. It became torrential, lashing them with stinging needles and snatching all the breath from Caitlin's body.

Jake shot out his hand and she accepted it gladly, feeling secure as his strong fingers clasped hers in reassurance. The squall hit, the wind screaming around them, and she kept stumbling in the gusts till he hauled her close to his body and timed his pace to hers so they moved as one person. Her hands were numb with cold, and water streamed from her saturated hair.

Jake forced her on when she would have sunk to a heap and let the storm do whatever it liked with her. There was a terrible stitch in her side and she clutched at it in agony.

'Not far!' he yelled at her.

She flashed him a despairing look and was startled at the elation in his eyes.

'You're . . . enjoying . . . this!' she gasped.

He grinned, the rain pouring down his face in sheets and then he laughed, the shock of his response making her catch her foot in a tussock of grass. If it hadn't been for Jake, she would have sprawled headlong. For a moment he held her steady, and she drew in great lungfuls of air as he sheltered her from the force of the gale, his eyes glittering brightly at her.

Then she was swept up, right off her feet into his arms, and he was shielding her face from the worst of the rain with a big, curving hand and striding strongly down to the harbour. Caitlin clung to the hard, resisting wall of his chest, intensely aware of the rock-hard tension of the muscles playing in his body as he fought to keep upright in the teeth of the gale.

Her arms slid around his neck and she tried to kick down a feminine delight in his immense strength and protective manner. Now the blast of the wind had lessened and she could tell from his easy strides that they were on level ground. Jake slid her to her feet, but she kept going as her knees buckled under her and she ended in a boneless heap on the grass.

'Up you come.' He grinned, his big hand yanking her to her feet again. He spread his hand in the small of her back, keeping her steady. 'Hell of a storm, isn't it?'

'You're mad!' she exploded. 'We're soaked to the skin and——'

'Better get to the boat, hadn't we?' he suggested, his eyes twinkling in amusement.

The rain had plastered his hair to his scalp and it lay like glistening ebony. The lines of his face were alert and vital, as if he'd been energised by the squall. He looked ready to burst with excitement.

Caitlin opened her mouth to demand that he let her go so they could board the launch, only to find it covered by his cold, rain-moistened lips, which grew warmer and warmer as the kiss grew longer and longer. Her arms twined around his neck again and she was oblivious of the rain still lashing down, only sensing the throb of his body and the answering beat of hers as she linked her fingers behind his head and twined them in his saturated hair. It was madness, a wonderful, uninhibited, wild thing to do.

He moved away reluctantly and gently pushed her towards the launch. Caitlin felt bemused by his kiss, and the way she had responded to him so naturally, not even caring that a force eight gale wailed about their heads, or that the heavens had opened above them. Jake was making her behave unconventionally, like him, she thought shakily.

Once on board, and in the comparative safety of the cabin, Caitlin felt comforted and reassured by the normality of her surroundings, and her cautious reserve returned.

Jake followed her into the cockpit and slid the glass door shut. Water poured from their clothes and puddled on the deck. Caitlin began to worry about getting home before they were chilled to the bone.

'How long do you think it will last?' she asked, peering out and avoiding his intense, watchful eyes. Desolate floods of grey water sheeted over the rock. She pushed her dripping hair back off her face and found it was stiff with salt from the spray that had been carried on the wind. In the outer harbour, the waves slapped together alarmingly, and she could see that the narrow entrance was a froth of foam where the sea lashed against the black, glistening rock.

'Ages.' He sounded pleased!

Caitlin frowned. 'Wait a minute—didn't you say that the weather would be perfect...?'

'For what I had in mind, yes,' he said calmly. 'The forecast said the squall would be followed by gales and torrential rain.'

She went cold. What exactly did he have in mind? An icy fear ran through her. 'You *knew*? You knew what kind of weather was forecast and *still* you brought me out here?'

'Correct. One of those opportunities not to be missed,' he said casually.

'You risked my life, you——'

'Oh, come on, Caitlin, I knew we had enough time to reach the island in safety and that the boat would be secure here. I only take calculated risks with myself—I wouldn't put you in danger. We got a bit wet; that's no problem.'

'I would rather be perfectly dry and at home than stuck on this island with you, cold and wet through,' she grated.

'Then we would never have advanced our relationship,' he commented.

'Oh, no! Think again! Our relationship isn't going anywhere. There won't even be any relationship, when I get back. I dislike being manipulated. I dislike arrogant men making assumptions. And,' she glared, 'I can't bear being manoeuvred into a position by men who imagine that a situation with no distractions and their wonderful, male proximity is going to make me fall into bed with them! If you think you're going to seduce me, you've another think coming!' she raged, inwardly tense with fear. Jake was strong enough to do whatever he liked. He'd planned all this, to make her a virtual prisoner, confined to the boat. They were completely alone and she had nowhere to run for help!

'Don't muddle me up with your ex-boyfriends. I'm not that kind of a bastard. I wanted us to have a long, uninterrupted time together,' he said quietly. 'There's a lot to get straight.'

'I don't believe a word you're saying. I'm not inexperienced in the way men look, and right at this moment you're weighing up your chances!'

She flicked back her wet hair defiantly. He wanted straight talking, she'd give it to him!

His lip curled. 'I know you're not inexperienced. And yes, I find this situation intensely arousing.'

Caitlin quivered at the huskiness in his voice as a small flame of fear and desire licked heat through her body, making her shiver.

'I find this situation intensely annoying,' she said icily.

'I'm sorry it's a scenario you've been through before. This one, however, will end up differently from the previous one,' he said harshly.

She bit her lip. Last time this kind of thing had happened—a carefully arranged isolation in a ski hut—she had successfully frozen out her eager suitor. This time... She shivered again.

'Before we start, we'd better get out of these wet things, first. Then we can get down to the reason I brought you here.' His eyes ran down her trembling body.

Her mouth fell open. 'You openly admit that you deliberately arranged this? Why, you...reprobate! You scheming, devious, infuriating...'

He grinned, quite unconcerned. 'Go down into the saloon and try not to soak the carpet. In fact, it would be better if you took your clothes off here. I'll turn my back. The shower is straight ahead, off the double cabin. I'll have a look and see what there is to wear. Contrary to what you're thinking, this was all rather spur of the moment stuff, and I'm not sure there's anything suitable.'

'Of course there isn't anything suitable!' she seethed, her teeth chattering. 'You don't want me wearing anything, do you?'

'To be honest,' he said, his eyes slowly touring her angry and tense frame, 'no, I don't. But I can see you're not ready for that idea yet, so——'

'Yet? Don't imagine I ever will be! I won't be abducted like this——'

'You came willingly, driven by your avid curiosity,' he pointed out. 'Caitlin, before I have to remove your clothes for you in order to prevent you catching pneumonia, please take a shower. I swear I'll do my best to find you something modest to wear, if I have to spend the next ten minutes redesigning the curtains.'

She glared at his amused face and grimly disappeared down the hatchway, squelching over the soft grey carpet and into a double cabin. As she slipped into the roomy shower, she heard him coming down the saloon steps and bolting the hatch cover behind him.

With a gasp, she slammed the shower door shut and locked it before wriggling out of her wet things. She was very cold. There was a scarlet towelling robe hanging on a rack. She turned on the shower. At least she had something to cover her nakedness when she finished, she thought, wondering what he intended to wear and trying not to think of his beautiful body. What a mess she was in!

The hot shower warmed her up considerably and she luxuriated in it, postponing the time when she had to face Jake. Slowly she rubbed herself dry and belted the robe tightly. Jake was in the saloon and he'd showered too, judging by the steam from his damp hair and the fact that he wore an identical robe.

'Yours suits you more than mine suits me,' he remarked.

Caitlin threw him a chilling look. 'Don't get any ideas,' she snapped.

As she moved cautiously to the comfortable silver-grey sofa, she caught a glimpse of a woman with a flushed face, her eyes sparkling like deep, lustrous pools, her lips a soft rose, parted over pearly teeth. The robe, which she had fondly imagined as covering her body like any ordinary piece of towelling, was so soft that it clung to her curves lovingly and the V of the neck revealed the beginning of the cleft that ran to her swelling breasts, outlined clearly as if meaning to be provocative.

She gasped at her reflection. Jake stared at her in the mirror, and she weakened at the simmering desire in his face. Then he turned and went into the galley. Caitlin drew in a deep breath, tugged the robe more firmly around her and arranged herself primly on the sofa. Jake confounded her by bringing in a tray holding a bottle of wine, two glasses, bowls of steaming soup, plates of smoked salmon, hot baguettes and grapes. Even more disturbing was the fact that he placed the tray on the low table in front of her and came to sit beside her.

She moved away from the hot pressure of his hip. 'For a spur of the moment entertainer, you certainly know where to find a late-night shop when you want one!' she said sarcastically.

Jake grinned and opened the wine. 'Everything came from the fridge, apart from the tin of lobster bisque, and I put that with the bread in the microwave. This is just what my friends left behind. They said there were some stores to be eaten up.'

'The microwave?' she asked faintly. 'Someone gives you an expensive launch with a microwave?'

His mouth quirked. 'Tuck in,' he said complacently, squeezing lemon liberally on the salmon. 'Be patient and all will be revealed.'

'That's what I'm afraid of,' she said sourly, contem plating a refusal of his seductive meal. But the soup smelt wonderful and greed won in the end. She decided there was no point in being hungry.

'The two men you saw on White Strand—I take it you *did* see them?' he asked.

Caitlin blushed. 'I saw four men in all,' she answered.

'Mmm. Well, two of them are incredibly wealthy. I saved their lives a little while ago and this is their way of saying "thank you". I must say,' he murmured, sipping his wine, 'it's a heaven-sent chance to get you alone.'

'Jake . . .'

'I won't hurt you, Caitlin, so take that startled look from your face,' he said seriously.

Perhaps if she could keep him talking, his desire would fade. 'Why were you so shaken when you saw them, if they're friends of yours?' she asked suspiciously.

'They'd told me they were intending to come over and bring me a small boat. When I saw the launch, I realised that their idea of small and mine are rather different,' he said laconically. Then he frowned. 'I had a fleeting memory of the last time we'd met, too. It wasn't in very pleasant circumstances.'

'What did you do, to save their lives?' she asked, swirling her spoon around in the soup thoughtfully. It sounded a far-fetched claim.

'I need to go back a bit, so you understand how I came to be involved. You see, I'd begun my working life in Africa, much of it in Angola as an agricultural adviser, though I discovered that anyone capable of living in a mahogany plantation doesn't need advice or interference, so I was left with time on my hands.'

'But what about your businesses?' Caitlin frowned.

'I inherited those from my father, I wasn't involved in them to begin with. Father was annoyed that I didn't want to get involved. I can stand desk-work for a while, but then I get itchy feet.'

She was right, he was a roamer. Jake reminded her of a gypsy, who never really put down roots. Whatever was he thinking of, taking on Cashel? Perhaps, if she stuck it out, he'd be gone in a few months and she'd be left there alone. The idea filled her with a feeling of emptiness. It ought to be an attractive prospect, but it wasn't.

'And then?' she prompted, taking a dainty bite from the crispy, hot baguette. It oozed butter and she licked her lips appreciatively.

Jake cleared his throat. 'Are you warm enough, Caitlin?' he asked solicitously.

'Yes,' she snapped impatiently. 'Get on with the story.'

'Pity. I hoped you'd be cold,' he murmured, his hand running lightly up her back.

'Don't!' she flinched, as her nerves responded by sending messages through her body.

'What a difficult woman you are.' He grinned.

'Just because you're used to instant success, don't imagine I'm like other women and find you irresistible,' she said coldly, her pulses hammering frantically.

'All right,' he said sadly, 'I won't. That leaves my life history, doesn't it? Well, I was chatting to someone in a bar in Luanda and had the idea of starting a Survival School, based on the knowledge I'd picked up living and working on the land.'

'A kind of jungle Outward Bound?' she suggested.

'More like Outward Dallas,' he grinned. 'I ran it originally for men in key jobs around the world who want to toughen up, or are in danger of kidnap, terrorist

attack, that kind of thing. With my government con-
tacts, the scheme got off the ground remarkably quickly.'

'So you ran this international Boy's Own fun camp
in Angola,' she prompted, unwillingly fascinated by the
kind of life he must have led. At least this was taking
his mind off her body!

'Right. And set one up in Tunisia, too. It suited me
perfectly. I'm pretty good at keeping my nerve. That's
how I manage to sit here and eat contentedly even though
the most desirable woman in the world sits next to me,
her thigh indecently close, naked under a wicked, sinful,
scarlet robe that keeps gaping, Caitlin, every time you
lean forwards!'

With a fierce movement, she sat bolt upright and
banged her fork down.

'Will you stop playing Casanova and act normally?'
she grated.

'That *is* normal,' he protested. 'The difficulty is in
trying to act abnormally and take no notice of you. It's
not easy. My heart's thudding like hell and it's taking
every bit of will-power I possess not to reach out and
slide that thing off your shoulders. I do so badly want
to kiss your shoulders, Caitlin,' he breathed appeal-
ingly, his lips soft and sensual.

She slid away from the table and went to stand on the
opposite side of the cabin. Her eyes flicked to the
porthole hopefully, but outside was dark, sheeting rain.
Did he think he'd talk her into bed? She bit her lip, upset.

Jake lowered his eyes. 'I'm sorry,' he apologised. 'But
I'm only human. You really are very beautiful.'

'Cut out the flattery. You promised to level with me
and I don't call this levelling,' she said in an icy tone.

'You're too damn controlled for my liking,' he muttered.

'And you're too uninhibited and sex mad for mine,' she retorted.

'Not compatible at all, are we?' he said, watching her intently.

She tried to prevent her mouth drooping at the thought and drew herself erect.

'This ghastly experience has been worth it if you realise that at last,' she said, meeting his eyes boldly. 'Tell me about your heroic act.'

Jake heaved a huge sigh. 'I admire your single-mindedness,' he said laconically. 'My heroic act, as you call it, came much later. I was just enjoying life, commuting between the two Survival Schools, when my father died. I hardly knew him, he'd always spent his time working, and never had much time for me,' he explained without self-pity.

Caitlin thought of him, without a mother, growing up independently of love. At least she'd had a great deal of affection up to the age of fourteen. No wonder Jake was heartless, with that kind of background.

'I suppose you inherited his businesses, then,' she commented.

'That's right. Despite my reluctance, I couldn't ignore my responsibilities to all the employees. I had to manage the companies. I sold some, kept what I could handle. Are you going to stand there for the next few hours? Come back, Caitlin. It's getting cold.'

She realised that she'd been shivering for a few seconds. 'Isn't there some kind of heating system?' She frowned.

'On a boat built in the tropics?' he asked. 'Come on, snuggle up to me. I'll pretend you're not a woman,' he teased, at her suspicious look. Feeling chilled right through, Caitlin allowed herself to be drawn to his warm chest and immediately felt cosier.

'You found out about Cashelkerry then, didn't you?' she asked, pretending not to notice the way his hand was massaging her arm.

'And that it was losing its value with every day that passed,' he said gently. 'You must understand, I had a powerful urge to return to the land of my forefathers, and an abhorrence of seeing good land mismanaged. I'd spent too many years trying to alleviate poverty in Africa to allow that. After I bought Cashel, I had an urgent phone call from a Tunisian. Two of his executives were being held as hostages by guerrillas in Angola. He'd been on my course and knew I'd worked there.'

He paused for a drink of wine. Caitlin was aware that all his bantering had ceased. In his face was a faraway look as he recalled what was obviously an unpleasant memory. As he talked, he held her tighter, cradling her to him—though not in a suggestive way. It seemed he needed comfort, and Caitlin put her arm around his waist and gave it a squeeze.

He patted her hand absently. 'I agreed to negotiate with the guerillas,' he said quietly. 'I got the executives out, but was taken prisoner myself, instead.'

She laid her head against his chest, hearing the rapid pounding of his heart. 'That was the prison you spoke of,' she said.

Jake had gone very still. 'More of a hell-hole,' he growled. 'They kept me in solitary confinement for about six months, in a small dark cave. I'd broken my leg and it had been badly set and drove me insane with the pain. Without it, though, I think I would have really gone mad. At least it gave me something to concentrate on. Eventually they'd investigated me and decided I was no threat to them and released me. It was months before I was strong enough to fly home. For a long time afterwards, I found it difficult entering dark rooms. I still shake a bit, going into caves and such-like. That's a difficult situation for me to accept—I dislike any form of weakness in myself. You ought to know that you're the only person I've told, Caitlin.'

She was intensely flattered. He trusted her enough to tell her about his fear. And then she remembered how he'd gone into the souterrain to rescue Danny, and how unnerved he'd been.

'I don't see it as a weakness. I see it as something you've been strong enough to conquer. You didn't hesitate to save Danny, even though it must have brought back terrible memories, being down that dark tunnel!' she exclaimed. 'Oh, Jake, you were even braver than I thought! You could have left him! What would it have mattered to you, if someone else's sheep-dog perished?' She turned her face to his, full of admiration for his selfless act. Jake, she thought dazedly, was turning out to be every bit the kind of man she'd wanted him to be.

'Don't praise me too much,' he smiled. 'Part of my actions are something to do with a fierce drive to get back to my normal state of having nerves of steel. I don't like being vulnerable.'

'I like it,' she breathed.

His eyes liquefied. 'How about some Irish coffee, Caitlin?' he murmured.

She nodded, but was reluctant to let him go. 'Don't take long,' she said huskily.

'Hell!' Jake paused in the act of pouring whiskey into each cup. His hand trembled. In the tense silence, he added hot coffee and concentrated hard as the cream slid down the back of the spoon into the black brew. When he returned to the sofa, his arm went automatically around Caitlin and she curled into him confidingly.

The warmth of the drink and the way it hit her stomach made Caitlin feel lazy and relaxed. Jake's fingers began to stroke her arm and she made no protest.

'I thought you were some kind of professional soldier or an international gangster,' she said, dreamily.

'And I thought you were superficial,' he countered. His hand reached around to cup her chin. 'But you're not, are you?'

Before she could answer, his lips had brushed hers, his eyes dark with smoky passion. The heat of his body was firing hers and, as they both lay back on the sofa, Jake hauled her on top of him, his hands sliding over her back and his mouth gently devouring her neck.

'You have such beautiful skin,' he breathed, his lips hot and incredibly arousing. He took her head in his hands and kissed her so tenderly that Caitlin's heart somersaulted with the sweet agony.

'I could do this all night,' he murmured, pushing back her silky hair.

'All night?' she cried, startled. 'Jake, we can't stay here all night, not together, not . . .'

'Of course we can.' He smiled, with a roguish twist to his mouth and a definitely predatory light in his eyes. 'We can hardly go anywhere. The weather is too bad for that.'

She remembered with a cold shock. Lulled by his story, relaxed by food and alcohol, she forgot that he'd intended to make her spend the night here with him, in the hope that she'd succumb to his masterly seduction. Master of Cashel! He'd taken her house, her land, and now expected to take her! He certainly believed in total victory. Well, she thought grimly, he'd miscalculated where she was concerned. No O'Connell woman was going to submit so easily. Jake Ferriter wouldn't be *her* master! She gritted her teeth against the treachery of her own bodily needs and tensed every muscle.

'Oh, hell,' groaned Jake, sensing her sudden frigidity. 'Don't go cold on me.'

Caitlin struggled to free herself and, to her intense humiliation, she wriggled too much and the front of her robe fell open so that her firm, smooth breasts tumbled out enticingly, their hard, dark pcaks betraying how much her body needed him, even if her brain was keeping her sane.

Jake's lashes flickered in thick, black fringes on his cheekbones, and then he dipped his head and gently took one nipple in his mouth, surrounding it with soft moistness and creating a startlingly erotic sensation that began its journey in the centre of her breast and ran like lightning to every inch of her body, until she was tingling down to her toes.

He was moaning in mounting passion, suckling her other breast, moving his body sensually beneath hers, and she whimpered, aware of his heat and his hardness, wanting to writhe her hips against him, to satisfy the overwhelming need within her.

'Caitlin, Caitlin,' he muttered, his tongue caressing and plundering her breasts in turn, 'I want you, you're driving me mad with desire. I don't think I can let you deny me any longer.'

'Jake——' she began.

'No,' he murmured throatily, his hands sliding over her thighs under the robe. 'No protests. Let me love you.'

She felt the delicate touch of his trailing fingers on her legs, and then he was cradling her small, tight bottom. Caitlin groaned at the effort it took not to tear his robe open and kiss every inch of his body.

A hand snaked to the back of her skull and pulled her head down on his, forcing fierce, hot assaults on her mouth that ground harder and harder until her lips felt bruised and yet longed for more to assuage the desperate emptiness filling her body.

Caitlin felt hazy, incapable of thinking clearly. Dimly she realised that she was naked, that Jake was murmuring something in her ear and his fingers were sliding between her legs. Frantically she squeezed them together, but he merely raised one knee and parted them, his touch rending from her a long, desperate moan.

With a quick, indrawn breath, Jake had skilfully rolled her on to her back, his relentless mouth driving into hers, his merciless touch forcing her breath to come in short, erratic gasps, turning her body into a melting, searing pool that liquefied and flowed into his hands.

'Ask me,' he whispered, savaging her lips in barely controlled passion. 'I want you so much. Tell me you want me too.'

His eyes sultry, he lifted himself slightly above her. Caitlin pressed her arms against his chest, pushing weakly. His dark head bent again to savour her breasts and she cried aloud as the knives of longing ripped her apart.

With a meaningful look, he lifted his head, his hand going to the belt of his robe. Caitlin's hand flashed down to stop him, and she closed her eyes in agony at the battle raging inside her. Nothing he had said suggested she was anything but someone who was conveniently on hand to give him a good time.

Her white teeth bit hard into her lip and she was aware that Jake had become very still, his muscles tensed. She shook with passion. Every inch of her skin seemed to be straining for his touch, his lips, the meeting with his body.

'I can't, Jake!' she said in a tone of despair. 'I can't give myself to you.'

'Why?' he asked harshly.

Her lids flew open. His face was suffused with the same agony as hers.

'Damn you!' he growled huskily. 'I can't walk away from you now!'

Tears welled from beneath her lashes. Her body began to quiver as she tried to suppress them. 'Please,' she whispered. 'You—you've gone too far. I didn't want——'

'You did,' he said bitterly. 'Oh, you did.' He thrust his hand through his hair in a bewildered, frustrated gesture and then he had stood up, tightening his belt savagely. 'Do you mind telling me,' he said in clipped tones, pouring himself a neat whiskey, 'if this is a temporary pause, if you're playing hard to get, or whether you never intend to include me in your list of lovers?'

Caitlin sat up in fury and saw his eyes kindle alarmingly at the sight of her angry body. Incensed, she grabbed her robe and covered herself, pressing it defensively to her, and glaring at him with baleful eyes.

'Don't be so foul,' she breathed.

'Can you blame me?' he snarled. 'You're experienced enough to know that you don't lead a man on that much and then go cold!'

'I'm not experienced!' she yelled, beside herself with a need for some kind of release. Like him, she wanted something she couldn't have. He wanted her with no complications, she wanted him and all the complications he could provide. But in her book that included love; it embraced tenderness and fidelity, something he knew nothing about.

He looked at her from under thunderous brows. 'Hell!' he exclaimed. 'Innocent you are not! You spend the last hour behaving more erotically than any other woman I've known, till even the slow flicker of your eyelashes becomes sensual, and you try to make out that you're not experienced? Come on, Caitlin, you know how to make love. You've just proved it.' He took a quick gulp of whiskey. 'Even the way you sit there, glowering at me,' he said quietly, his voice thrilling her with its sensuality, 'arouses me incredibly. Just being near you is an aphrodisiac.'

A hard lump rose in her throat, preventing her from speaking. Her hands trembled and she felt her breasts swelling, just to his words and the husky way he spoke. There was no doubt that he desired her, and it was intensely exciting to think that she could arouse such a worldly, sophisticated man as Jake.

She flinched and shot him a warning glance as he put down his glass and took a step towards her.

'Caitlin,' he said softly, 'we are alone on this boat. We'll be here all night. Soon it will get very cold. We're both still hot, from passion, but that won't last if you persist in freezing me out. Let me get another bottle of wine and we'll sit for a while and chat.'

'No. I don't want you near me,' she said doggedly.

'I understand why you're doing this,' he began.

'You do? Why?' she frowned, clutching at the robe.

'Because you're still harbouring some resentment. I took Cashel from you. What you must remember is that it wasn't yours in the first place,' he said gently.

'Where are you going to sleep?' she asked icily, ignoring his words.

'With you,' he answered remorselessly. 'Fight all you like, protest all you wish, but finally we'll end up in the same bed. Maybe the double bunk through there, here on the sofa, or on the floor. It doesn't matter. I'm not going to take "no" for an answer, Caitlin. This situation is impossible for me to bear, and I see no reason for two hungry adults like us to act like innocent kids. You have no reason to refuse me. And I intend to make love to you. I've held back for too long.'

Her almond eyes showed her fear. He walked towards her, fixing her with his hypnotic gaze, and Caitlin felt herself falling under its spell.

CHAPTER EIGHT

Shock-waves of pleasure coursed in disturbing ripples through Caitlin's brain and body at the dangerous, intensely erotic hunger emanating from Jake.

'Why do you persist in pretending to yourself and me that you don't want this?' he growled softly. 'I have every intention of showing you how much I need you.'

He paused and the intoxication of his eyes bewildered her. She was afraid. Afraid of the fierce emptiness within her, his masculinity; terribly uncertain how to crush the deep internal throb that vibrated every nerve and caused her skin to suffuse with a glowing colour.

'Jake,' she said hoarsely, holding up her hands in a defensive gesture, 'I am perfectly aware that you could rape me if you wanted——'

A frown caused his brows to meet. 'Rape? How can you think that? I'm talking about sex. Seduction. Lovemaking.'

'I don't want that,' she said in an undertone. 'I can say it over and over again, if you like, but it seems you won't listen. You are so certain, so arrogant, so darned sure of yourself, aren't you?' she ended, vehemently.

'I...' His face stilled. 'I don't understand,' he breathed.

'No,' she said, managing to sigh as if irritated. 'Men who are supremely aware of their own sexuality never do.'

'Perhaps you'd explain,' he said tightly.

Caitlin blinked and she thought rapidly. Inside, her heart was breaking at the look of misery on his face, but it was a stupid reaction on her part. He was only upset that his sexual adventures were being curtailed for the night.

'It happens so often to me——' she began, remembering the countless men who'd imagined themselves to be irresistible. Though none of them were, whereas Jake almost was.

'I thought so,' he growled.

Her eyes flickered up at him and met his scornful gaze. All right, so he believed she often led men on; his hatred was safer than his lust.

'It seems to take rather a long time for some men to get the message,' she said, only just controlling her voice.

'Now I do understand,' he said grimly. 'You're a sexual tease. You enjoy the preliminaries, but are so frigid that you're scared to go the whole way. Is that right?'

She reeled under his baleful glare. 'I suppose,' she said slowly, thinking he was half-right, 'I suppose that's about it.'

'Of all the women I have to get stuck with in a luxury boat for the night, it has to be you,' he grated. 'Thank heavens there's more than one cabin. Unless you've got any other ideas, I suggest we get some sleep. I'll ring Cashel, in case they're worried about us.'

'Ring?' cried Caitlin. 'Are you telling me there's a phone on board?'

'There's virtually everything on board, except a normal, healthy woman,' snarled Jake, storming off to the cockpit.

His exit left her feeling like a limp rag. She flopped on to the sofa and closed her eyes weakly. Tonight she was safe. In fact, her virtue was probably safe for the rest of her life! She really couldn't imagine ever wanting any man as much as she wanted Jake. Apart from his chauvinistic treatment of women, he was everything she admired. Between them was a sexual chemistry that couldn't be denied. If she—as he had so cruelly pointed out—was a normal, healthy woman, she would have melted into his arms and let the future take care of itself.

As it was, he had made it clear that he wasn't a man who stayed in one place for long. Caitlin curled up, listening to his voice on the phone. She gave it a year before he became bored and began looking for new excitements. A year in his arms would bind her to him so strongly that she'd never want to give him up.

She couldn't bear to see him grow restless in her company, to start making excuses and stay out all night. He'd have a ready-made reason: that he was training. She swallowed, imagining his deceit. He couldn't help it; he was just a rover. No woman could hold him.

He padded down the steps and Caitlin averted her eyes from his naked, muscular legs.

'I'm going to bed,' he said, without looking at her.

Miserably she watched him stalk into the bow cabin beyond the galley and slowly dragged herself along to the double bed, trying not to think of the kind of night she might have had, if she'd allowed herself to become his willing victim.

The morning was wet and grey. Jake silently prepared breakfast of fruit and toast and then they watched television. Gradually the bad weather cleared and he announced in a remote tone that they could leave. Caitlin waited until the launch was safely through the harbour entrance before going in search of her clothes.

Although Jake said he'd been trying to dry them over the oven door, they were still soaking wet. She visualised them walking up to Cashel House, dressed in matching towelling robes, and groaned!

Unwillingly, she climbed up to the cockpit, rubbing her arms from the cold up there. Jake was at the wheel, his uncompromisingly angry back to her.

'Jake...'

'What?' he snapped.

'We can't turn up like this!' she said anxiously.

'Don't worry,' he said, his gaze sternly ahead. 'No one would imagine you'd done anything in the least bit sensual.'

'Swine!' she cried.

'Cormac is bringing us some clothes,' he growled.

'*Cormac?* Oh, Jake, how could you?' she said, appalled.

His cynical eyes swivelled to her horrified face and he gave an unpleasant laugh. 'So he was something to you, after all.'

'No, it's just that... I'll be so embarrassed...'

'Not half as embarrassed as you would be trying to keep your robe from flapping open in the wind as we walk home,' he said sardonically.

Caitlin's fists clenched in helpless rage. 'That was particularly mean of you,' she said tightly. 'You could have asked Brigit...'

'She's shopping. It's market day. Besides, he's already there. Look.'

Ahead, she could see Cormac's big shape and the topping of red hair standing on the jetty. Without a word, she went down to the saloon. In stiff expectation, she sat waiting. The boat's engines cut out and there was an exchange of greeting, then heavy feet landing on board. She didn't look up when someone climbed down the steps, not wanting to see the accusation and contempt in Cormac's eyes.

'This is yours.'

From beneath her lashes, she stole a quick glance and saw only Jake, holding out a carrier bag. She stretched out an uncertain hand.

'Cormac?' she asked.

'He's gone on. Don't be long. Or are you going to change in here with me?'

Caitlin let out an impatient sniff and fled into the cabin, slipped into the underwear and track-suit and only emerged after a cautious call from her evoked no response. Jake had already dressed and was moving around above.

'Let's get home,' he said when he saw her.

Home. That was the second time he called Cashel that, she thought rebelliously. It was only a pit-stop for him.

'What did you tell Brigit and Cormac?' she asked, as they walked back.

'That we'd been caught by the squall, that we'd had a foul, uncomfortable night, we'd had one hell of a row and I couldn't wait to get back,' he said grimly.

'Why did you tell them we'd quarrelled?' she asked irritably.

'To make it quite clear we hadn't been loving the night away,' he snapped. 'I was trying to protect you.'

'Thanks,' she said coldly. 'I don't need your protection.'

'No,' he said, his face harsh. 'I don't believe you do.'

*   *   *

If it hadn't been for the fact that she knew Jake would one day leave, Caitlin would never have stuck it out over the next few weeks. In order to maintain an aloof and cool image, she reverted to her old style of dressing, in elegant suits and a carefully made-up face.

Brigit tried to talk to her about Jake once or twice, but Caitlin made it clear that she didn't want to discuss him. Work on the house had almost been completed and the Survival School was expected to begin its first course in the spring. Already it was booked up months in advance. At least when Jake left she'd be fully occupied, she thought glumly.

One morning, just before Christmas, she was arranging flowers in the hall, coolly efficient in a tailored blue wool skirt and a prim blouse, when there was the sound of a car outside. Jake emerged from the study and ran across the flagstones, flinging open the front door.

A beauty with a cap of shining raven hair ran into his open arms and was whirled into the air. Under Caitlin's shocked eyes, the woman wrapped her arms around Jake's neck and kissed him hard on the mouth.

'Oh, you darling!' she cried huskily, hugging him tightly. 'It's wonderful to see you. I wish I could have come over earlier. Trust you to leave me with the job of running Tunisia!'

'You're the only person who could do it, Louella,' said Jake, in a fond tone which made Caitlin bristle. 'We started the place together, after all. Come on in. I'm so glad you're here. We have a hell of a lot to catch up on.'

'I haven't heard the whole story of your capture yet——' she began. 'Oh, hello.'

Caitlin smiled politely.

'This is Caitlin O'Connell,' said Jake, keeping his arm around Louella's waist. 'Meet Louella Seymour. You two have something in common.'

'Have we?' laughed Louella, slanting a laughing glance at Jake.

'Wicked woman,' he grinned affectionately. 'You're both perfect hostesses. Which room do you think, Caitlin?'

Her eyes flickered. 'I'll check,' she said calmly, intending to put her in one as far away from Jake as possible. This was the same husky-voiced woman who had booked the long-house for Jake. She was certainly on very intimate terms with him.

'No, don't bother,' he said lightly. 'Have the one next to mine, Louella. We can stay up all night eating and watching old films again.'

Caitlin bit her lip and turned away as they both made to go upstairs, totally absorbed in each other. She saw Cormac standing by the kitchen door, following Louella with his eyes.

'Wow,' he breathed. 'Who's that gorgeous woman?'

'Part of Jake's harem,' she said tartly, and found she was still holding chrysanthemums in her hand. She banged them down on the kitchen-table.

'Dammit,' complained Cormac. 'Why does he get all the best-looking women?'

'Because he's so obviously a swine,' she said crossly. 'And some women like a challenge.'

'You really despise him, don't you?' he said.

'Yes, I do,' she answered with great feeling.

'Miss Seymour will be staying a few days,' said Jake, making them both jump.

Caitlin glanced pointedly at his soft-soled shoes and tipped up her chin proudly. She didn't care if he knew what she felt about him.

'I thought she might,' she said without expression.

'She's a very good friend of mine and I want you to make her welcome,' he said in a warning tone.

'That's my job, isn't it?' she said brightly.

His mouth twisted and he left, the memory of his cynically mocking eyes burning into Caitlin's brain.

The house was filled with their laughter—and Cormac's, because he managed to tack himself on to them a great deal. Caitlin spent as little time in their company as possible, though she did have to work hard not to like Louella; she was very lovely and eager to be friendly.

Too friendly towards Jake. Caitlin had heard Louella's distinctive giggle one afternoon and glanced out of the drawing-room window, only to see her rolling in the grass with Jake, her lovely, breathless face flushed and happy.

Bolts of pure jealousy tore through Caitlin's body as she turned away and gripped the back of a chair for support. Tears started in her eyes and her upper lip trembled. How much longer was she going to be tormented? A low groan escaped her and she flashed a tortured look at the couple, still tangled like playful lovers.

'Something wrong, dear?'

Caitlin turned her back on Brigit and pretended to be adjusting the drapes. 'No,' she said in an unnatural tone, and decided to say nothing more in case she betrayed herself.

'Tut. What a way for a grown man to behave,' chided Brigit affectionately. 'Sure there's nothing wrong?' she probed. Caitlin shook her head, unable to turn because of the stinging tears and wishing Brigit would go away.

'Louella isn't what you'd call a shy woman, is she?' mused Brigit.

Caitlin didn't care what Brigit thought: she couldn't stand it any longer, hearing the laughter outside, and imagining the playful touching, the embraces... She rushed from the room and stormed up the stairs, slamming her door hard and throwing herself on the bed in a frenzy of weeping. When Brigit came up shortly after and knocked timidly on the door, Caitlin muffled her sobs beneath a pillow and kept a tight rein on herself until she gave up calling anxiously.

That evening Caitlin didn't appear for dinner, and Jake came up to see why she had been delayed.

'Caitlin?' The door rattled. 'Let me in! Caitlin, are you all right?'

Reluctantly, seeing from the way he was shaking the door that he wouldn't be satisfied until he had an answer, she slid from the bed and hastily controlled her weeping.

'For heaven's sake, leave me alone!' she cried fretfully. 'I have a terrible headache and all you can do is yell.'

'I'm sorry,' he said, lowering his voice a little. 'What can I get you——?'

'Nothing!' she exclaimed, her nerves jangling. 'Leave me alone.'

His footsteps died away and she lay miserably on the bed again, unable to sleep, unable to do anything but imagine Jake and Louella, making love. She thought of his eyes melting with desire, his sultry mouth descending to Louella's, and bit her lip in agonised distress. What a fool she was, letting Jake upset her! She'd known ever since he first arrived that he was a seducer. If she was going to picture him in bed with every woman he touched in her presence, she'd never be able to get on with her life.

She had to pull herself together. She had to prove to herself that she could forget Jake. There must be other fascinating, sexy men in the world who weren't out and out rakes. And if not—well, she'd stay single and make sure she made a life that didn't include fickle men.

Caitlin grew more remote, more cool towards everyone. She could just about tolerate the way Jake placed his arm around Louella and escorted her into dinner. It was possible to obliterate from her mind the times that she had heard the sound of Louella's laughter and a man's muffled voice downstairs, late at night. But it wasn't easy to fall asleep, nor could Caitlin pretend to be cheerful.

To her dismay, Jake and Louella had decided that they'd throw a party on Christmas Eve, and had invited many of their friends. Jake had also invited some of the local people and all his work-force. The four of them spent hours decorating the house, wreathing it with garlands, and it looked wonderful. For Caitlin, it was a bitter-sweet time, her antagonism towards Jake modified into a polite truce, his proximity quite unnerving on occasions.

He seemed to go out of his way to be left alone with her, to taunt her by reaching across her, or lifting her down from a step-ladder quite unnecessarily. Several times she'd snapped at him irritably and he'd just smiled in his infuriating way, probably delighted that he'd annoyed her.

Louella, Brigit and Caitlin were putting the finishing touches to the buffet, set on the lovely fruitwood table in the dining-room, when Jake called in to tell Louella that there was a phone call from Tunisia for her.

'Oh! My darling Ahmed!' she cried, and whirled off in a cloud of delicate perfume.

Jake grinned at her retreating figure and came in, beginning to check the table.

Brigit gave a disapproving sniff. 'I didn't know she had an Arab boyfriend as *well*,' she said, folding napkins.

'Louella?' Jake laughed. 'Now, you know very well that she's fallen madly in love with Cormac.'

'What did you say?' gasped Caitlin. What deceit was he practising now? Even to Brigit it must be obvious that Jake had captured Louella's heart.

'If you spent more time with us, instead of hiding in your room, you'd know,' muttered Jake. 'Does the idea upset you?' His eyes glittered, green and wicked.

'Why should it upset Caitlin?' puzzled Brigit.

'The thought of losing Cormac,' explained Jake. 'I think he's serious—and I know Louella is.'

'You and she . . . I saw . . .' She bit her lip. If she protested that she'd seen them rolling in the grass, that would hardly sound as if she was indifferent, and it would make her feel undignified remarking on his outrageous behaviour.

'You're thinking of that time Mr Jake and Miss Louella was fooling around on the lawn,' nodded Brigit.

Caitlin wished the ground would swallow her up.

Jake frowned. 'Fooling . . . oh!' He grinned. 'Stupid woman.' He smiled fondly, his faraway expression telling Caitlin that he meant Louella. 'She insisted on wearing those spindly heels. Served her right when she fell over and ruined her suit. Cormac was mad.'

'I'm sure he was,' said Caitlin with asperity. 'If he imagined he was the only man on the scene.'

'No, I mean she was on her way to the Register Office, to fill in forms or whatever you do,' he said innocently. 'She didn't have time to change you see. She met Cormac there and had the devil of a job explaining her muddy skirt.'

'He's not totally trusting, then,' remarked Caitlin.

Jake laughed. 'You saw what happened.'

'No, I didn't,' she said stiffly. 'I don't like to intrude on lovers' games.'

'Silly,' said Brigit. 'They wasn't lovers' games. They just giggled and got up. Mr Jake doesn't feel that way about her, not...'

'Thank you, Brigit,' he said hastily. 'Nice, isn't it?' he added to Caitlin. 'The idea of wedding bells?'

'Are you seriously telling me that they're thinking of getting married?' asked Caitlin, unable to believe her ears.

'Yes, I am. Ahmed is just a friend, like me.'

'There,' said Brigit, wagging a finger at Caitlin. 'See what interesting gossip you miss by going off to your room. I hope you're not moping. That doesn't do any good.'

'I have no reason at all to mope,' she said tightly. 'I don't love Cormac and never have. If he's happy...' She thought of the way he'd begun to sparkle lately, and smiled, realising why. And of course, while Jake had taunted her, Louella and Cormac had been thrown together. How lovely. 'Well, I'm very glad. He's a really nice man.'

'I didn't mean you were moping for Cormac...' began Brigit.

'Please!' muttered Caitlin, seeing Jake was becoming interested in their conversation.

'Hmm. You know what I'm referring to,' said Brigit meaningfully. 'To be honest, I was afraid that you'd inherited your father's attitude.'

Caitlin's eyes filled with pain at the blunt words.

Jake forestalled her protest. 'What do you mean, Brigit?' he murmured absently, carefully decanting the red wine.

'She didn't mean anything,' put in Caitlin hastily.

'Yes, I did,' insisted Brigit, not understanding tact. 'He had Cait's emotions,' she said.

'Oh, yes?' encouraged Jake.

'He loved as hard as she does,' said Brigit, missing both Jake's alert expression and Caitlin's tight mouth and fierce fingers as she twisted the napkins into shape. 'Only one other man I've seen look at a woman, the way Seamus O'Connell looked at his wife.'

'Really?' said Jake in a bored tone. 'So what do you mean about his attitude?'

Brigit put down the glass she was holding and leant forwards over the table in a confiding manner.

'They were so happy together, an ideal couple. When she drowned, it was as if part of him had been cut out, the feeling part. He took to his room and started drinking. This poor child knew nothing of that. All she was aware of, was that her father grieved. You didn't know, did you, Caitlin?'

'No,' she whispered. 'Not till near the...the end. If I had, maybe I could have done something...'

'I doubt it. We all tried,' sighed Brigit. 'He gave too much of himself.'

'It's a mistake,' mumbled Caitlin.

'No, it isn't!' denied Jake vehemently. 'It's a mistake to keep your emotions locked up——'

'If you mean Caitlin, she had to, Mr Jake,' defended Brigit. 'To begin with, she couldn't cry for her mother and Patrick, she was numb with shock. Then her father couldn't bear her trying to take her mother's place and sent her away to fiddle-faddle about in Europe. Every time she came back and tried to get things shipshape, Seamus O'Connell sent her away again. She looked just like her mother, you see. She did her best, but it wasn't too good because Seamus kept interfering.'

'Do you think he deliberately ran the estate into the ground?' asked Jake in a strange voice.

'No, he loved it too much! It was the drink, fuddling his brain, poor, lovely man that he was. He hid from Caitlin a lot of the time so she didn't see him drunk, he was that ashamed. But I knew that she cried in secret——'

'Brigit!' wailed Caitlin. 'This is my personal life!'

'About time you shared it,' she said sternly.

'I don't want it discussed in the presence of the man who caused Father to die,' breathed Caitlin.

Brigit shook her head. 'Your father set himself on that road, when he first took a bottle of poteen to bed. It affected his brain.'

'I mean the phone call. He had a heart attack after that,' she said huskily, trying not to cry. Why, oh, why had all this been dragged up, a couple of hours before the party? How on earth could she appear calm and carefree?

'That was nothing to do with me!' cried Jake angrily.

'You two, you do get heated!' said Brigit, her face flushed. 'Now I never told anyone this, because I thought I should keep my mouth shut about things that don't concern me. But your father talked to me long and soberly just before he died, asking me what I thought was best for you. He said he was going to ring Mr Jake and ask him to take over Cashel, that he realised he shouldn't try to hold on to it any longer.'

'Father wouldn't do that! He'd never agree to anyone throwing me out!' cried Caitlin.

Brigit laid a hand on her trembling shoulder. 'He was going to ask for you to be given a home here until you found a husband and left to get married,' she said. 'We both decided it was for the best. If Mr Jake didn't get that call, it was only because Mr O'Connell died before he could make it. Of natural causes, Caitlin, made worse by the drink.'

In misery, Caitlin shut her eyes and Jake came over to put his arm around her waist.

'I think I ought to take you to your room. Have a lie down and come to the party if and when you feel up to it,' he said gently. 'Can you manage, Brigit?'

'I certainly can.'

'Thank you. I'll change and come down as soon as I can to give you a hand. Cormac and Louella will, too, if they can tear themselves apart from each other.'

Caitlin allowed herself to be led upstairs, feeling bewildered. Jake would have been Master of Cashel whatever had happened! She sat on her bed dully, while Jake drew the curtains. He knelt down and slipped off her shoes, lifted her feet and swung her legs around so that she lay on the bed. She felt frail and small and very miserable.

'I'll leave you now,' said Jake in a choked voice.

Utterly exhausted, she slept. The room was very dark when she woke, and it was a moment before she remembered it was the night of the party. Faint sounds of revelry drifted to her ears. She'd have to go down, it would look so peculiar if she didn't, and she refused to let her emotions beat her. She'd conquered them before, she could do so again.

Like a zombie, she stripped and stepped into her dress. As she zipped up the slinky, white full-length dress, which hugged every curve of her body, she stared at herself. There was no life in her eyes. Her dejected posture made the slender and fragile straps slip off her shoulders, so she had to draw herself erect.

Hastily she renewed her make-up and carefully applied some blusher, and a strong colour on her mouth to hide her pallor. She could do nothing about her eyes. As she descended the sweeping stairs, she tried hard to bring life into her expression.

In fact, her face did soften at the scene and a feeling of pleasure tugged at her heart. The spacious hall was bright with evergreen and red ribbon, the tall barley-sugar shaped red candles casting a golden, flickering glow over the people milling around, chatting, drinking, laughing. It was as Cashel House should be and, for that, Caitlin was grateful to Jake Ferriter.

Still she hesitated. It had been a long time since she'd walked into a gathering like this. The women were all beautifully groomed and expensively dressed, the men immaculate in dark suits. They all seemed so confident and, since her emotions had been plucked from her body by Jake, she had become less sure of herself.

'Hey!'

There was a shout from one of the men below, who'd seen her, a slender, curving and elegant figure in white, her beautiful and somehow secretive face inducing the single men below to hurry to greet her. Suddenly Caitlin was surrounded by a sea of faces, all introducing themselves. To her, the men who had pushed themselves to the fore were all a little like Jake, in the way that they had that expression he wore when his adrenalin was running, eyes glittering with excitement, face glowing in the peak of health.

Protesting mildly, she allowed herself to be borne into the drawing-room and its festive scene. At the sight of Jake, leaning easily on the mantelpiece as if he'd been Cashel's owner all his life, she tried to stop the inexorable journey to his side. He was in a circle of glamorous women, all vying to be treated with a glance from his dark eyes, a flutter of his thick lashes and a word from his cynical, sexy mouth. To Caitlin, he dominated the room and she felt her pulse-rate increase alarmingly.

'Wait!' She forced a laugh and pleaded with the men. 'I'm breathless!'

'This is the time to take advantage of you, then,' grinned one.

'I'll protect you,' urged another. 'Now, outside, I happen to have a pure white steed, ready...'

'In this weather, you'd prefer a Lamborghini, wouldn't you?' murmured a tough looking man on her left.

'If I said I'd hired the QE2 for the weekend...'

Caitlin was amused at their banter—and flattered that they should flirt with her so obviously. Perhaps she did look all right. It might not be such a bad evening at all, especially if she could steer clear of Jake and keep a cool head. But he had seen her, excused himself from the conversation and was striding over.

The men around Caitlin chattered eagerly, admiring her openly and making suggestions so outrageous that she didn't feel threatened at all, only a friendliness towards them for boosting her confidence so much. Yet she was intensely aware of Jake who was heart-wrenchingly handsome in a perfectly cut dark suit, white shirt and scarlet tie.

The men, who had previously shouldered away amiably any others who had tried to join the group, parted immediately they saw Jake. Though they did grumble, much to Caitlin's amusement.

'Trust you to come and spoil everything!'

'Hell. Shouldn't you be checking the wine cellar, or something?'

'Telephone call for you, Jake, from Luanda.'

Jake gave them all a mocking glance, but his eyes were gentle when they reached Caitlin.

'You are the most beautiful woman in the room,' he began.

'Ireland. Tell her, Ireland,' broke in one of the men.

Jake silenced him with a glare. 'Thank you for coming down, Caitlin. I'm afraid you'll need nerves of steel to cope with this lot.'

Despite his sour look around the group, Caitlin knew that these were men he'd worked with, and that there was a close bond between them. In fact, from the way they looked at Jake, she could tell they would probably fling themselves off cliffs for him. She lowered her lashes so that no one would know she'd fallen under his spell, too. Seeing him in Cashel House tonight, surrounded by his friends, she felt such love for him that she couldn't be bitter any more. It was one of those things; it wasn't his fault he didn't love her, he could hardly be blamed because she couldn't reach his heart.

'Since you are my hostess, I think we should open the dancing,' he said.

'That would be lovely.' She smiled, raising her shining eyes. His expression shook her to the core. He looked... Caitlin blinked away the thought and composed herself as Jake led her to the ballroom. Her hand was trembling in his. Or was his shaking, too? she thought wildly, her mind a ferment of contradictory messages.

He drew her into his arms and it was as if they melted together into one person, gliding around the floor oblivious to anything but the rhythm of their bodies and the thoughts in their heads. They danced without speaking. Jake held her close, the curves of her body meeting the hard, toned muscles of his, and she felt deliciously feminine and increasingly sensuous as they dipped and swayed to the music.

One hand rested on his broad shoulder, shifting a little to pleasure itself in the feel of his back, the other was clutched tightly in his big fist, and pressed against his chest. She could feel his erratic breathing softly fluttering over her tiny ear and the exposed nape of her neck, and she was so sensitised to him that she knew of the increase in the rate of his breathing as they toured the floor. He pressed her more tightly to his body and they swayed in one fluid movement.

The music ended. Jake slowly drew away, leaving her with a bereft sensation. He smiled and led her back, Caitlin hazily noticing that the floor was filled with couples. Other men claimed her for dances. She was passed uncomplaining from one to another, struggling to keep up a semblance of normality, while all the time her brain reeled.

What her instincts were telling her was impossible. Jake was just being kind—putting on a show for the guests, pretending to be interested in her so that she was protected from unwelcome advances. Those messages in his eyes couldn't be what she thought they were. Men like Jake Ferriter weren't fool enough to fall in love, they just had a good time.

Throughout the evening, talking, sampling the buffet, dancing, their eyes kept meeting. Caitlin didn't intend that to keep happening, but it did. On every occasion that they looked away from each other, she vowed not to look again, and immediately found herself catching his eye once more.

He seemed more sober than anyone else, more silent, and ever watchful. Towards the end of the evening, her nerves were strung taut. She stood at the base of the stairs to say goodbye to guests who were leaving, and Jake manned the front door, seeing them off into the dark night. Then the house suddenly echoed with Jake's final goodbyes and she realised everyone was gone.

Everyone, that was, but Cormac and Louella, who were deep in an embrace under the mistletoe behind her. She smiled and went to slip past unnoticed, but Cormac stopped her.

'We're so happy for you, Caitlin,' he said warmly.

'You are?' she asked, puzzled.

'We certainly are,' agreed Louella, giving her a hug and a kiss. 'Now excuse me. I squeezed into this darn dress and I've been breathing in all night. I just *have* to slip into something more comfortable. And if you think that's an invitation, Cormac Kelly, you're darn right. See you in a few minutes.'

Their amused eyes followed her up the stairs. Cormac held Caitlin's shoulders and looked up at the mistletoe with an enquiring smile. She stepped forwards and he gave her a gentle kiss.

'Enjoy yourself,' he said cryptically, and thundered up the stairs after Louella.

Caitlin had the sensation of being watched. She slowly turned and looked over her shoulder. Jake had shut the main door and was standing in a slightly threatening way, his eyes piercing hers.

Jake began to walk towards her.

She felt her heart fluttering as it beat against her rib-cage, and without thinking she strode blindly into the dining-room, picking up a plate and selecting morsels of food. Every inch of her body was conscious of the fact that he had followed.

'Hungry, Caitlin?'

The way he said that, in a sultry and liquid voice, meant she couldn't answer 'yes'. It would sound as if she knew he was talking of a different hunger—and he was right, she thought wildly, her body tightening in an effort to contain her desire.

'*That* hungry?' he persisted.

She looked down on her plate. It was so full that the pile of food was tipping slowly to the floor. Jake took the plate from her nervous fingers, then swivelled her around. His arm reached up high, and Caitlin saw that he held the bunch of mistletoe in his hand.

'Jake...'

'Pagan custom,' he murmured. 'Can't be resisted.'

His gentle mouth enclosed hers, softly moving, sweetly destroying all her vows and all her defences. The kiss went on for ever and ever. Languorously Caitlin lifted her arms and twined them around the nape of his neck, and Jake's hands slid down to her waist, fitting perfectly in the curve. She felt her body begin to bend back as her mouth began to murmur her pleasure, and Jake's lips grew more demanding. Then she was being hauled upright and their lips eventually reluctantly parted.

Jake stroked the hollow of her cheek.

'Let's go somewhere more private,' he said huskily, his eyes burning into hers.

A wave of dismay deadened her pleasure. 'Oh, Jake,' she said sadly, 'I've told you so many times! I don't want sex in that way!'

'That's not what I'm after. Well, yes, I am, but—oh hell! You've got me in such a state, I don't know what I'm saying! Caitlin, I want us to talk.'

'We've done that,' she said wearily, staring at the knot on his tie.

'Not this kind of a talk,' he said seriously. 'It's a final one.'

Final. Realisation flashed through her mind. He intended to tell her that she could either play the willing partner in his bed, or get out. He dealt in blackmail, used every opportunity. He wouldn't miss this one—it must be so obvious to him what she felt now.

Well, she thought miserably, it had to come. Better get it over with. She'd see if Mrs Murphy would let her stay with her for Christmas.

'In the study,' she assented in a dead tone.

'In the drawing-room.'

Her eyes flashed a warning. 'You might think that's a better place to seduce me, with its comfortable sofas, but it won't make any difference!' she grated.

'Caitlin, desks, sofas, carpets—it doesn't matter. If I want seduction, it can be anywhere.'

'Like outside the drawing-room on the grass, with Louella!' she blurted out, consumed with jealousy.

'She's Cormac's girl!'

'You wouldn't let a little thing like that stop you!'

'Here.' He caught her elbow and grimly marched her into the drawing-room, pushing her into an easy chair and surveying her darkly. 'Stop being so stubborn. You know perfectly well you were wrong about Louella. Don't you think you might be wrong about imagining my continual interest in other women? That, in fact,' he continued angrily, 'there were no others at all?'

'I'm sorry, Jake,' she said stiffly, not enjoying this a bit, 'but I can't accept that a man as highly sexed as you could remain celibate.'

'I may have mentioned that I'm determined. I see something I want and I make sure I get it, even if it means a period of self-denial. Since I met you, Caitlin, I haven't even been interested in another woman, let alone made love to one. You were on my mind all the time. You still are,' he added, in a low, throaty tone.

She raised spiky lashes to him, searching his face dubiously. Everything she saw told her that he was sincere. But...

'It won't work,' she said quietly, aching from the pain her words were causing. 'You are a roamer. You crave excitement, danger. Soon you'll be bored with Cashel and want to leave.'

He knelt beside her and took her hands. 'I don't know what to say to convince you about my intentions. I could say that I want to stay here forever, that I've found in Ireland the kind of people and the kind of country that makes me feel I belong. I could say that Cashelkerry has so much scope that it would take a lifetime before I was bored, especially with the sunsets and the colours, the scenery and the wild life. I might tell you that I love you and will go on loving you forever. But after that, you'd have to trust me, believe in me.'

'You—you'll find it dull here,' she gulped.

'Dull?' he laughed. 'It's going to be non-stop action if I have my way.' His mouth twitched. 'I'll be shinning up and down cliffs in the dark——'

'No! I wish you wouldn't!' Caitlin's face expressed her alarm.

'Trust me. I'm an expert,' he murmured, his mouth incredibly tempting. Caitlin fought to stay sane. 'We'll have those dinner parties and bandy words with Arabian princes, development engineers, pop stars, actors and wealthy business men and women. We'll wander into Dingle and lean on a cobbler's bench and pit our wits in conversation with the Irish people there. How am I doing?' He grinned, seeing how soft her face had become. 'Then the action switches to the bedroom.'

'Jake—I told you——'

'Caitlin, I'm trying to tell *you*. This is my home. My roots are here. Inside me, I know I want to stay here for the rest of my life. I can run all my companies from Cashel. I need never leave. We need never be apart. Excluding short absences down cliffs, and during night manoeuvres, that is,' he teased. 'I love you. I think I fell in love with you the first time I saw you, sitting on that dry-stone wall with your skirts spread all around you—a mysterious, elusive and unattainable woman.'

'You asked me to be your mistress . . .'

'I wanted you for myself. I was so jealous of your jet-setting boyfriends. It was an attempt to persuade you that one man could give you more pleasure than many. Especially if that man cared for you deeply.'

'My reputation is entirely exaggerated. But . . . I think you'll discover that truth for yourself in time.'

Caitlin's heart somersaulted at the way Jake's breath caught in his throat at her suggestion, and her lips parted in delight. Jake loved her. She searched his eyes, to be certain, and saw anxiety and love there, all mixed up. She disentangled her hands, smiling at the alarm on his face, and reached out for him, gasping as he hugged her so tightly to him that she could hardly breathe.

He held her for a long time, their hearts beating in unison. Then he whispered in her ear. 'You know I said I didn't want to leave Cashel?'

Caitlin's body froze. From his tone, he was already reneging on his earlier statement!

'Well,' he murmured, kissing her ear, 'I was thinking of a trip to Mustique.'

She tried to tear herself away, but he struggled with her, laughing. 'You beast,' she raged. 'Let me go! I won't . . .'

Her mouth was captured, plundered and made prisoner by his wicked lips, which left her breathless.

'My darling,' he breathed. 'We have to go *somewhere* for our honeymoon.'

'You devil!' she complained, trying not to laugh. 'How dare you tease me like that?'

'I have to make some effort to appear master in my own house,' he mused. 'I am so madly in love with you that you might take it into your head to twist me around your little finger.'

'No woman could do that to you,' she answered with a smile. 'Certainly not one who loves you as much as I do.'

His long finger traced the outline of her mouth tenderly. 'Hell, the Irish have done it again,' he said ruefully.

'Done what, Jake?' Caitlin asked, kissing the line of his cheekbone.

'Subdued a foreigner in the arms of one of their women. Now I know how my ancestor Piaras felt!' Then he was kissing her again, as if he couldn't get enough of her mouth.

Outside, the moon silvered the grass and the distant rolling waves. It lit for a brief moment two storm petrels, in their fast, sure flight to the island. The moon's rays gleamed on White Strand, on Cashel's pastures, the lake and the Crag with its romantic ruin.

And, in the secure warmth of Cashel House, Jake Ferriter was happily lost in Caitlin's arms, a stranger no more and now as blissfully absorbed with his Irish sweetheart as any of his ancestors.

HARLEQUIN
Romance

Coming Next Month

Available in August wherever paperback books are sold, or through
Harlequin Reader Service:

In the U.S.
901 Fuhrmann Blvd.
P.O. Box 1397
Buffalo, N.Y. 14240-1397

In Canada
P.O. Box 603
Fort Erie, Ontario
L2A 5X3

THE LOVES OF A CENTURY...

Join American Romance in a nostalgic look back at the Twentieth Century—at the lives and loves of American men and women from the turn-of-the-century to the dawn of the year 2000.

Journey through the decades from the dance halls of the 1900s to the discos of the seventies ... from Glenn Miller to the Beatles ... from Valentino to Newman ... from corset to miniskirt ... from beau to Significant Other.

Relive the moments ... recapture the memories.

Look now for the CENTURY OF AMERICAN ROMANCE series in Harlequin American Romance. In one of the four American Romance titles appearing each month, for the next twelve months, we'll take you back to a decade of the Twentieth Century, where you'll relive the years and rekindle the romance of days gone by.

Don't miss a day of the CENTURY OF AMERICAN ROMANCE.

The women...the men...the passions...
the memories....

CAR-1

You'll flip . . . your pages won't!
Read paperbacks *hands-free* with

Book Mate • I

The perfect "mate" for all your romance paperbacks
Traveling • Vacationing • At Work • In Bed • Studying
• Cooking • Eating

Perfect size for all standard paperbacks, this wonderful invention makes reading a pure pleasure! Ingenious design holds paperback books OPEN and FLAT so even wind can't ruffle pages – leaves your hands free to do other things. Reinforced, wipe-clean vinyl-covered holder flexes to let you turn pages without undoing the strap . . . supports paperbacks so well, they have the strength of hardcovers!

Pages turn WITHOUT opening the strap

SEE-THROUGH STRAP

Reinforced back stays flat

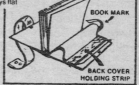

Built in bookmark

BOOK MARK

BACK COVER HOLDING STRIP

10 x 7¼ , opened
Snaps closed for easy carrying, too

Available now. Send your name, address, and zip code, along with a check or money order for just $5.95 + .75¢ for postage & handling (for a total of $6.70) payable to Reader Service to:

Reader Service
Bookmate Offer
901 Fuhrmann Blvd.
P.O. Box 1396
Buffalo, N.Y. 14269-1396

Offer not available in Canada
*New York and Iowa residents add appropriate sales tax.

BM-G

Harlequin Superromance®

A powerful restaurant conglomerate that draws the best and brightest to its executive ranks. Now almost eighty years old, Vanessa Hamilton, the founder of Hamilton House, must choose a successor.
Who will it be?

Matt Logan: He's always been the company man, the quintessential team player. But tragedy in his daughter's life and a passionate love affair made him make some hard choices....

Paula Steele: Thoroughly accomplished, with a sharp mind, perfect breeding and looks to die for, Paula thrives on challenges and wants to have it all ... but is this right for her?

Grady O'Connor: Working for Hamilton House was his salvation after Vietnam. The war had messed him up but good and had killed his storybook marriage. He's been given a second chance—only he doesn't know what the hell he's supposed to do with it....

Harlequin Superromance invites you to enjoy Barbara Kaye's dramatic and emotionally resonant miniseries about mature men and women making life-changing decisions. Don't miss:

- CHOICE OF A LIFETIME—a July 1990 release.
- CHALLENGE OF A LIFETIME
  —a December 1990 release.
- CHANCE OF A LIFETIME—an April 1991 release.

SR-HH-1

COMING SOON

In August, two worlds will collide in four very special romance titles. Somewhere between first meeting and happy ending, Dreamscape Romance will sweep you to the very edge of reality where everyday reason cannot conquer unlimited imagination—or the power of love. The timeless mysteries of reincarnation, telepathy, psychic visions and earthbound spirits intensify the modern lives and passion of ordinary men and women with an extraordinary alluring force.

Available next month!

EARTHBOUND—Rebecca Flanders
THIS TIME FOREVER—Margaret Chittenden
MOONSPELL—Regan Forest
PRINCE OF DREAMS—Carly Bishop

DRSC